The Blood Room

The
Blood Room

Christina Hoag

Three Jandals Press

The Blood Room
Copyright 2021 by Christina Hoag
All rights reserved.

ISBN: 979-8-9871887-1-2

Published by Three Jandals Press
Santa Monica, California
United States of America

This book is a work of fiction. Names, characters, places and incidents are the product of the author's imagination or are used fictitiously. Any resemblance to actual events, locales, or persons, living or dead, is coincidental.

Also by this author

Fiction

Skin of Tattoos
Girl on the Brink
Law of the Jungle

Nonfiction

*Peace in the Hood:
Working with Gang Members to End the Violence*

1

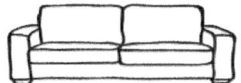

He'd been branded like a steer. Los Angeles Police Detective Desi Nimmo leaned in to examine the wound. She held her breath out of force of habit although she'd already taken the precaution of daubing her nostrils with Vaporub.

Under the raw festering mess, the injury on the man's upper left buttock had a discernible shape—oval, maybe three inches by two inches big, with a horizontal line across the center. Curious. She snapped a picture of it with her phone.

Hector, the coroner's tech, pointed to a red streak like a comet trail on the man's hip before replacing the bandage. "Looks like the wound went septic," he said.

Desi ran her eyes over the full length of the body: male, white, twenty-five to thirty-five years old. Dressed in a fashionable shirt and jeans, polished loafers. Definitely not the homeless transient that she'd expected early that morning. She'd received the callout of city sanitation workers finding a stiff on an abandoned couch in a West Los Angeles alley.

His eyes bulged in a shocked stare, the whites firm and round as hard-boiled eggs. Death had pounced on this guy like a highway robber.

"So sepsis could be the cause of death," she said.

"We'll find out. There's also this." Hector rucked up the man's shirt to expose his back covered with red polka dots amid the purpled lividity. Some had scabbed over.

"Those look like burn marks. Cigarettes," she said.

"And this." Hector hiked up the legs of the guy's jeans. His sockless ankles were encircled with bracelets of bruises. "Maybe a week old."

"Wrists?"

Hector picked up the arms. They displayed the same pattern of contusions.

He'd been tied up, branded, burned. Tortured. But he'd been walking around for a while with the wounds.

"ID?"

"He's a John Doe. No wallet or phone on him," Hector said.

It was a complicating factor, but this was a guy who would be missed sooner rather than later. His identity would turn up.

"Time of death?"

"Six to eight hours ago, give or take. He was likely running a fever when he died, which makes body temp a little hard to gauge. He died here on the couch. No visible signs of drug use."

"Detective Nimmo?"

She wheeled toward the baritone voice that boomed behind her. Cheap mud-colored suit, lightly salted hazelnut hair combed back. Cop. He stuck out his hand. She shook it warily. Who the hell was this?

"Finbar McNab, Fin. Transferring to West LA with the new DP today. The LT asked me to come over and assist. I've been a murder cop for the past seven years. Newton."

Desi knew he'd added the last part to emphasize his bona fides. Newton Division had a handful of homicides per month as compared to West LA's handful of homicides per year, if that. The implicit putdown scraped her.

"It's under control," she said. "No assistance needed. It'll be up to the slice and dice to determine if there's anything to investigate."

The lieutenant had mentioned they were getting a new guy at the previous week's squad meeting. She'd also said he'd be a floater, that Desi, as the major crimes detective in the bureau, could assign him where needed.

And that wasn't here.

McNab craned his neck to take in a vertical view of the victim's back as the coroner's techs lugged it onto a gurney and into the waiting body bag. "Those wounds don't look like an accident or natural causes."

She returned his quizzical look with a flint-edged stare. "Suspicious death." She squeezed out a smile to punctuate the conversation with a period and shifted her gaze to the row of stores that backed onto the alley.

The sun's first rays washed the landscape of low-rise urban sprawl with pale clarity. She normally reveled in the sliver of dawn that impregnated the new day with possibility, but she now felt intruded upon by this newcomer.

"TOD?" he said.

"It'll be in my report," she snapped then regretted her tone.

The lieutenant had probably dispatched him to the scene to give him something to do. She'd give him something else back at the station. She had a stack of cases that she hadn't had time to do much work on since her partner had died. She relented.

"Between eight and ten last night."

Desi looked back at row of businesses. The Pen & Ink Café was the only business with a light on in its rear window. She could use coffee. She'd skipped that crucial step when she'd bolted out of bed in pre-dawn darkness.

She turned to two uniforms standing around bullshitting. "Let's get a strip search going. One of you at the east end of the alley, the other at the west. We're looking for a wallet, cell phone, keys, drug paraphernalia. Check the couch."

The officers shifted to opposite ends of the alley and started trudging back and forth across its breadth, sweeping the ground with their eyes, sifting through tufts of weeds growing along the fence, checking the Dumpsters.

"I'm going to the coffee shop," Desi said.

"I'll play Tonto," McNab said.

"You know *tonto* means dumbass in Spanish?"

"I said I'll play Tonto, not that I am *tonto*."

So he was asshole who thought he was a smartass.

They headed into the café through the back door. It was one of those trendy places with raw-wood paneled walls that sprouted tufts of greenery from built in planters. The aroma of coffee sliced the air as the espresso machine whooshed and hissed.

A twenty-something woman was already at a table banging away at her laptop, the blocks of Courier text on her screen the giveaway that she was working on a movie script. Westside coffee shops made a fortune off aspiring screenwriters.

As Desi ordered a latte, the middle-aged barista, her silver-streaked hair in plaits, eyed the gold shield clipped to her belt.

"LAPD?"

"Yep."

"What's going on out back?" She tamped the coffee into the espresso basket and flicked the machine's switch. "It was blocked off when I tried to drive in this morning."

"Someone died back there," McNab said.

"Not the old homeless guy who's always sleeping on that couch?"

"It turned into a deathbed for a younger man. Were you working last night by any chance?" McNab asked.

The dude was a real buttinsky. Desi glared at him, but he kept his gaze trained on the barista.

Either he had peripheral blindness, or he was pointedly ignoring her. Likely the latter.

"Yep, one of the perks of being the owner. I'm here from opening to closing, nine-thirty."

Right at the estimated time of death.

"Did you happen to see anyone on that couch or in the alley last night?" McNab continued.

Desi felt a swell of anger. "Do you mind?" she said to McNab as the barista turned to pour the coffees.

McNab threw up his hands in surrender. "Hey, just doing what they pay me to do."

Pigtails twisted back to them. "No, can't say I did. When I left, I threw the trash in the Dumpster and got in my car, but I've seen the homeless man out there before."

The door swung open and a younger woman, her face a confusion of freckles, rushed in.

"The alley's full of cops. They have crime scene tape up," she said in a breathless voice. "It took me ages to find street parking."

"A guy died there last night," the barista said over the hiss of foaming milk. "A young guy, not the old homeless man."

The girl's eyes saucered. "I saw someone lying on that sofa last night when I left, but I thought it was the homeless guy." She ducked under the counter and disappeared into a back room. She reappeared a moment later, draping an apron over her head.

"What exactly did you see?" Desi asked.

"She's a cop," Pigtails interjected.

Desi swung back the flap of her jacket to display the shield.

The younger woman looked thoughtful. "You know, there was a dude who seemed sick in here last night. He went to the bathroom but come to think of it, I didn't see him again. I wonder if it was him."

"What time was this?"

"Not long before closing. He was sitting with a girl. He got up and bumped into a lady and spilled her coffee. He looked sick or strung out. I asked him if he needed help. He shook his head then he staggered to the back. The lady was freaking out about the spilled coffee so I had to deal with her and get her another one. He might've gone out the back door. We keep it unlocked."

Desi took out her phone and punched up the photo of John Doe's face. "Sorry to have to show you this, but is this him?"

Her hand leapt to her mouth. "Oh my god."

Judging by the barista's reaction, Desi had found a witness. "Is this the man who was in here last night?"

"That's him, I'm sure of it," she said.

"What about the girl he was sitting with? What did she do?"

"She just sat there. I was kind of surprised she didn't help him."

"Can you describe her?"

"She had her back to me. All I saw was a ponytail, dark brown or black hair."

The barista's name was Adriana Hochstetter. Desi thanked her for her help and handed her a card with the usual instruction to call if she remembered anything else.

Two coffees were waiting on the counter. "Sorry, we don't have doughnuts." Pigtails beamed at her punchline.

"Do I look like I eat doughnuts?" Desi said. The barista's face fell. Desi dug into her pocket and took out some crumpled bills.

"It's on the house," Pigtails said.

"Thanks, but it's against policy." Desi set down the money, grabbed the cup and headed toward the back door.

"Don't mind her. Bad morning," McNab said behind her.

Fuming at McNab's nerve, Desi exited into the alley, halting in the anemic sunshine to sip the coffee. It was lukewarm. They never made it hot enough. The burn of hot coffee sharpened her brain as much as the caffeine. McNab shuffled up beside her.

Desi rounded on him. "Listen, Mac-whatever-it-is. This is not your case. I did not request your assistance. And you have no fucking idea about my morning. Got it?"

"Whoa. I apologize if I stepped on your sensitive toes. And it's McNab, by the way."

He wandered over to the uniforms. Desi took a deep breath and pushed him out of her head. She had bigger things to worry about.

John Doe had taken ill. He'd gotten up to go to the bathroom, but maybe it was occupied, or he just wanted fresh air. He'd gone outside, spotted the couch, lay down for a spell. And never got up.

The sight of a uniform and McNab huddled over a plastic evidence bag broke her reverie. For fuck's sake. She marched over.

"What have we got?"

The officer handed her the bag. "We found it under the Dumpster next to the coffee shop door."

A key chain with an electronic fob bearing a Porsche emblem. That fit with John Doe's overall style. Several house keys. A large one, likely a master key to an apartment building front door. She examined the key chain itself. A silver-dollar sized circle with a logo of two chevrons forming a diamond. "TeleBank" was inscribed in silver letters under it.

She pressed the Porsche fob and listened. Nothing. She walked to both ends of the alley and stood on the sidewalk, clicking the unlock button. No beeps or flashes. She returned to the patrol officers.

"I want a BOLO on a Porsche parked in the vicinity. As soon as the body snatchers leave, you can clear the scene."

Another patrol officer barreled up the alley, a smooth-cheeked woman with her hair pulled back tightly in the regulation bun. "Detective, we got a suspicious device alert. We've been ordered to evacuate the block."

2

Desi's senses pricked to alert. Could there be a connection between the body and the suspicious device?

"Where is it?" she said.

"The bus shelter at the corner of Wilshire."

Desi relaxed and rolled her eyes. "You gotta be shitting me." She marched toward Wilshire Boulevard.

A black-and-white patrol car was parked haphazardly on the street, blocking traffic, which was starting to rev up for the day.

In another hour Wilshire would become as clogged as the arteries of a fast-food junkie and stay like that until long past nightfall.

A patrol officer on the sidewalk redirected the few pedestrians. Flashing her shield, Desi walked past him.

"Bomb squad's on its way," he called.

She peeked into the bus shelter. As she'd thought. A banged up old suitcase was chained to the bench with a bicycle cable lock. In this era of terrorist paranoia, everything became a possible bomb, but she knew who put it there.

She returned to the two officers. McNab now milled next to them.

"Call a code four and get a pair of bolt cutters," she said.

"Don't you think we should let the bomb squad do its job?" McNab said.

"The suitcase belongs to a transient, Sal Belvedere. He chains his junk up all over the street all the time, especially on the first of the month when he gets his general relief check and goes on a binge."

"Someone could exploit that by turning a suitcase into an IED," McNab said.

"A terrorist who hangs out with homeless people to gather intel? You can stand on the other side of the street if you're worried about my judgment."

"Just saying." McNab shrugged.

A bluesuit returned with a bolt cutter. McNab took the tool from him and walked over to the bus shelter where he poised it open-jawed over the bicycle lock.

Showoff, Desi thought.

"You sure about this?" he said.

"Yeah. It's happened before when they put a new car on the sector."

"If not, I'll come after your ass in cop heaven."

He snipped the lock with a flat clack. Desi pulled out Latex gloves from her jacket pocket, wriggled her hands into them and opened the case.

A jumble of items tumbled out: a bouquet of faded plastic flowers, brittle-paged paperbacks, a sheaf of folded documents bound with a rubber band, a kazoo, faded photos in a wrinkled envelope.

She picked up the papers and showed the name "Salvatore Belvedere" on them to McNab.

"You called it," he said. That was his peace offering.

"Clear," she yelled to the uniforms, then turned to Fin. "Let's canvass the businesses for any surveillance footage of the street or alley last night."

"Roger that."

Finbar McNab walked across the parking lot to the police station's rear entrance. Ahead of him, Desi Nimmo swung the door open and entered. The door banged closed behind her. It figured he'd wind up with one of these women cops with the personality of a thistle and a name like "Nimmo" as part of his "punishment."

No matter. He'd had to deal with colleagues like her in the past. He wouldn't be sticking around the West Los Angeles division for long anyway.

He took a deep breath and ascended to the detective squad room on the second floor. It was small as squad rooms went and badly in need of a makeover. The windowless room was furnished with clusters of old metal desks and filing cabinets sitting on a floor of cracked linoleum.

All that was missing were the old "table" nameplates hanging from the ceiling on chains designating the sections: narcotics, juvenile, property/auto theft, major crimes. The place was obviously neglected by downtown, which was depressing on several counts, notably for his prospects for promoting out of there.

As he entered, Desi turned from a conversation with two other detectives clustered around a desk.

"Have you met anyone yet, McNab?"

She'd used his name. That was a positive sign. "Just the lieutenant," he said.

Nimmo turned to the other cops. "Finbar ... Fin, right?" She questioned him with her eyebrows, and he nodded. "... McNab, starting today from Newton. This is Keisha Hardy. She works our sex crimes table." She gestured to a high cheek-boned woman who unfolded herself from her desk to a height of almost six feet.

"And in-demand prostitution sting decoy," chimed in a mustached guy hiking up his pants under a bowling-ball belly. "She pulls so many johns we're thinking of charging a fee to other divisions—prostituting the decoy. Larry Stamos, narcotics."

"And wannabe standup comic. With the emphasis on wannabe," Desi said.

"Guess I'm going to have to work on that punchline," Stamos said.

"Just forget the whole damn joke." Keisha shook his hand. "Glad to have you aboard. We're all working cases solo because of this hiring freeze. It's hit us hard."

"Newton's down a bunch of people, too, but it's a much bigger squad," Fin said.

He had done his homework on his new assignment. Geographically, West Los Angeles was the biggest of the LAPD's twenty-one divisions.

It covered sixty-five square miles and a population of three hundred thousand people, including some of the world's most famous faces and the obscenely rich who lived in neighborhoods such as Bel-Air and Holmby Hills. Institutions like UCLA and Fox Studios brought an additional two hundred thousand people a day to the area.

For Angelenos, West LA was the epitome of the city's notoriously clogged traffic. For the LAPD, it was a "low activity" station with little violent crime known derisively as "West Latte." For Finbar McNab, it was a demotion.

Still, he empathized with his new colleagues. The squad was barebones for such a big population, and that meant ballooning case backlogs and sinking morale. Typical LAPD.

"So how come you transferred from Shootin' Newton?" Stamos fired the question that Fin knew would be on everyone's minds.

Fin felt sharp points of his new colleagues' six pupils. He shrugged in pretend nonchalance and rolled out his rehearsed response.

"Just wanted a change of pace. Been working homicide for seven years." Bullshit answer. He knew what they were thinking: Freeway therapy, the LAPD brass's favored strategy to oust troublemakers.

Punish them with a transfer so they'd have a long-ass commute and eventually quit. But if the West LA squad didn't already know why he was transferred, he wasn't going to tell them.

It was just a matter of time before they found out anyway. Once lit, the cop grapevine crackled like a dynamite fuse.

"You have your choice of desks." Desi gestured to empty work stations as she sat at a desk and powered on a computer. Was it his imagination or was she being a little nicer to him?

The desk next to hers looked empty, and he needed to stay close to the major crimes detective if he was going to bounce out of this purgatory to the Robbery Homicide Division, the handpicked squad of detectives that exclusively worked high profile and complex cases and his dream since he was a pepperoni-faced fourteen-year-old.

But making RHD had now become more than fulfilling a childhood fantasy. He had to show the asshole brass at Newton, who had drummed him out of there based on one mistake without even considering his fourteen-year, blemish-free record, that he didn't need them.

And he had to show Ginger, that traitorous bitch, that despite her desertion of him at his biggest time of need, he was doing better than ever without her.

But he had to have a case as his trampoline, a big one that was going to stand out and get attention, but not too big, like some Michael Jackson-style celebrity where RHD would swoop in automatically and swipe it.

Who knew, maybe this John Doe could be it. Maybe his luck had finally turned, and on the first day of his new assignment, no less. He felt a twinge of optimism, the first in a long time.

He pointed to the desk. "This open?"

"That was my partner's," Desi said.

" 'Was' meaning he's not coming back?"

"Not from where he went." Desi paused. "He died eight months ago, cancer."

So she'd been working solo all this time. No wonder she was a ball of prickles—and as territorial as a Southside gangbanger. "Sorry to hear it. I'll get going checking on that bank name on the key chain," he offered. "That could be where John Doe worked."

"Actually…" Desi grabbed a handful of manila folders from a tower on her desk and handed them to him. "…if you could go through these unsolveds for leads, I'll handle the John Doe."

He took the folders without a word and yanked the knot of his tie loose as he flipped open the top one. Grunt work. Desi Nimmo would be tough to crack. He was going to have to find a way to push things along, and he did not have time to waste. He needed to wedge himself in on the ground floor of this suspicious death. It might be the best thing he could get in West Latte for a while.

Ten minutes later, he looked up from reading the file on a six-month-old armed robbery of a 7-Eleven and spotted Lt. Evangeline Butler's considerable backside emerge from her office and waddle toward the staircase. He hesitated as an idea came over him. He had to admit, it was pretty shitty. Then again, he owed nothing to nobody. He had to look out for himself. Nobody else was going to. He waited two minutes, which seemed an acceptable interval, then trotted downstairs.

Fin looked around the station's ground floor but couldn't see the lieutenant. He waited a minute, then he spied her coming down the hall from the roll call room. He looked around as if he were searching for something.

"Hey, Lieutenant. Locker rooms are on this floor, right?"

She halted and shook her head. "Basement. How's it going so far?"

"Great. I met some of the other detectives, but I guess I stepped on Nimmo's toes this morning. It looks like a possible homicide, but she didn't exactly appreciate my help. Now she's got me trying to heat up a frozen two-eleven."

He hiked his shoulders as if to say, "Oh, well."

"I'll handle it."

"No, I really didn't mean …"

"Don't worry. I'll take care of it." She hauled her bulk up the stairs.

Fin smiled and hurried down to the men's locker room.

3

The search of California DMV records for John Doe's fingerprints came up empty, which meant he was probably an out of-stater. It was common enough. Everyone in LA, it seemed at times, was from somewhere else.

A request to run the prints through the FBI's national database would take time. No print matches on criminal records. Ditto with missing persons and nothing had shown up from the be-on-the-lookout for the Porsche.

Desi also searched for any police reports alleging torture, kidnapping, or false imprisonment over the past month. Nothing. John Doe couldn't have been treated at a hospital or they'd have reported injuries like those.

He obviously hadn't seen a private doctor, either, or he'd gone too late. That may have been why the wound went septic. But he must've been in pain, felt generally sick. If he hadn't sought help, he'd been afraid of questions about how he got the wounds.

Desi turned to the keychain. She'd searched the internet for TeleBank and found that it was an investment bank in downtown LA. She called, and after some dithering by the receptionist, was put through to the vice president of human resources.

Moira Reed promised to make inquiries about employees missing keys, or an absent employee, or maybe even a client fitting John Doe's description.

"We think he could drive a Porsche," Desi said.

"That *could* narrow it down." The woman's voice oozed doubt.

Desi hung up, shaking her head. Must be nice to spend more than an average cop's annual salary on a fancy toy. She noted the time. The library had opened. She could return Sal's suitcase.

As she stood and pulled out the suitcase from under her desk, McNab's head jerked up like a marionette pulled by a puppeteer.

"Where are you headed?"

"Going to return the transient's suitcase."

"Want some company?"

"I'm good."

McNab leaned back in his chair. "That barista said a homeless guy always slept on the couch. Could that be your guy?"

"That's what I'm going to ask him."

Desi eyed him. McNab didn't miss much. He also seemed to have a keen interest in the John Doe. It wasn't much of a case, although better—and fresher—than the stale burglaries and holdups she'd just given him. The downturn of his mouth hadn't escaped her when she'd handed him the folders. Well, too bad, buddy.

As Desi was scribbling her whereabouts on the sign-out board next to the door, Lt. Butler stuck her head out of her office door.

"Desi, come on in for a minute."

The lieutenant probably just wanted an update on the body. Still the less Desi had to do with brass, the better. "I'm just heading out."

"It'll only take a minute."

Desi followed Butler into the office and sat in front of the desk as the lieutenant lowered herself into her executive black leather chair. Butler stuck to rules and regulations with the force of Super Glue, but Desi respected her.

It couldn't have been easy for Butler, starting at the LAPD over a quarter-century ago, to promote through the ranks. Sticking to the rules was the safe way up. Then nobody could make her a target. Police Politics 101—the essential course they didn't teach at the academy.

Butler leaned forward on her desk. "What's the deal with the body this morning?"

"A John Doe. He was tortured, looked like he was branded."

Butler flinched. "Branded?"

"Yeah, like with a hot iron. I'm waiting on the cut to determine cause of death, but I'm going on the theory that he died of his injuries, in which case we have a one-eighty-seven."

"I tell ya, you've never seen everything in this line of work." Butler shook her head and steepled her hands. "I want you to work with the new guy on it." She glanced at a paper on her desk. "McNab."

Desi's gut pinched. "LT, you said at the squad meeting that he was going to be a floater."

"That was before I reviewed his file. Homicide's his thing. We need to take advantage of his expertise. That's why I sent him out this morning."

"You think I can't do it on my own since Burke left, is that it?"

"Not at all. It just makes sense to have McNab as your partner, especially if you've already caught a homicide. If it gets slow, I can assign him to whoever needs help. Got it?"

Desi took a deep breath. "Roger that. Anything else?"

"That's all," Butler said.

Desi exited the lieutenant's office, feeling as if she'd slipped on a rug corner and almost taken a tumble. Did McNab beef her to Butler for that bullshit about not waiting for the bomb squad? She caught herself. She was being paranoid. The bottom line: she was now stuck with him.

She had to make the best of it. They'd didn't have to be buddies, just establish a working relationship. And maybe the LT was right. She should use his expertise. Plus, she had to admit, it got lonely working cases solo.

She was used to having Sam Burkehalter to bounce things off. Even after he went out on sick leave, she'd call him up for advice.

He'd been more than a partner. He'd been a mentor, a coach. It had helped that he was gay.

After what she'd gone through in Hollywood Division, a non-threatening male had been exactly what she'd needed to get her mojo back.

Now she was back with a typical LAPD male alpha ego.

She walked back to the desks. "Hey, McNab. You're coming with me."

Fin looked up in surprise then jumped to his feet, snatching his jacket from the back of his chair as she pivoted on her heels.

"The library's half a block away. We're walking," she called over her shoulder.

He caught up to her as she pulled open the front door of the station lobby and launched into a brisk stride. "Let me do the talking. Like I told you, I go back a ways with Sal," she said.

"He a CI of yours?" Fin asked.

"Unofficial. I met him when a couple of his buddies OD'd on bad smack. After I nailed the dealer, he's given me a hand from time to time. He knows the local transients. He helped me find a couple of unregistered sex offenders we were looking for."

They rounded the corner onto Santa Monica Boulevard. Desi waved at a cop in a cruiser who stopped to let them cross the street.

"Listen, I'm sorry about this morning," McNab said. "The LT told me to go out there. I didn't mean to…"

Desi sliced through the apology, not wanting to hear it. "Don't worry about it. It took me by surprise, that's all."

"Slate cleared then?"

"Slate cleared."

They halted in front of the library.

Desi took out the Vaporub from her jacket pocket and daubed her nostrils. "You wait around the side of the library with the suitcase. I'll go find Sal and bring him out." She tossed him the Vaporub. "His perfume can be overpowering."

"Thanks for the heads-up."

Desi entered the lobby, where a motley bunch of overstuffed shopping trolleys, carts and bursting bags was parked under a sign banning "oversize items," and headed straight for the bank of public computers.

She spotted a head with a thundercloud of matted grey hair in a booth. She pulled up a chair next to him. His eyes were riveted to a skin flick with the sound muted.

"Hey, Sally," she said in a low voice.

He darted his eyes at her and turned back to the screen. "'Sup, Desi."

"You miss anything lately?"

"Like?"

"Your suitcase."

That nabbed his attention. "You got my case?"

"Let's go outside."

"I'm gonna lose my booth. I'll have to wait hours to get one again."

"Which is more important? Getting your case back or porn? I'll meet you round the side of the building. No one will see us."

As Sal pulled himself to his feet, Desi darted ahead. She found McNab standing in a well of sunshine at the appointed spot, the suitcase at his feet. At least he followed direction.

"He's coming," she said. "Had to pull him away from a porno movie."

"That can't have been easy."

Sal lumbered around the corner. "How'd you get my suitcase?" He scrunched his eyebrows at McNab.

"This is a colleague of mine, Fin McNab. He's okay," Desi said. "Patrol called your bag in as a suspicious device early this morning. The bomb squad was on its way. It almost got confiscated and destroyed."

"I can sue them for that, you know. There's court cases about taking homeless people's property. They got no right," Sal said.

"I need to ask you something. You know about a couch in an alley behind Wilshire?"

He frowned. "Shit, that got called in, too?"

"You go by there last night?"

He averted his eyes. "Nope."

"Sally, I saved your ass today, bigtime. I stuck my neck out for you 'cos you and me got history. So come on, tell me the truth."

Sal rubbed the cleft in his chin and studied the suitcase from under the hood of his eyes.

"Don't you even think of trying to grab that suitcase or I'll put a robbery charge on your ass," Desi said.

On cue, McNab stepped over the suitcase, so it was behind his legs. Sal said nothing.

"Let's go, McNab." Desi bent to pick up the case.

"I saw him," Sal blurted. "He was in a real bad way. I figured he OD'd."

Despite his disheveled appearance and drug-addled brain, Sal was no dummy. He once told her he'd been a union shop steward at an aeronautics plant in the South Bay in another life, pre crack cocaine.

She straightened. "You roll him?"

"Hey, he was already dead. And he was having himself a good ol' time with his chickie on *my* couch."

"What do you mean?"

"I seen a woman with him. She got up and walked away when I yelled at her to get off my couch."

Desi felt a hard edge lace her gut. A woman who walked off and let a man die? Who never even called 911? She was at the very least a witness, or at most a suspect. Either way, they had to find her.

"What did she look like?" Desi asked.

Sal scratched his chin. "Long hair, dark, pulled back. That's all I seen. She walked away real fast. I didn't catch her face or nothing. It was dark."

"What time was this?"

Sally shrugged. "Nighttime, not late."

"You sure he was dead?"

"He wasn't movin' when I got to him."

"So where's his wallet and phone?"

Sal shook his head. "Got there too late. The girl cashed in and scrammed. Can I have my stuff? Told you all I know."

"You saw her take his shit?"

"Well..." He scratched a bristled cheek. "I really just seen her sitting."

Desi studied him. If he was lying about robbing John Doe, the wallet and phone were long gone by now. She picked up the luggage and set it down at Sal's feet.

"Don't leave it chained up in public again. You can take it downtown to that place where they store belongings for homeless people."

"They'll just jack my stuff." Sal snatched his case.

She started to move off then heard Sal behind her.

"Hey, Desi, you ain't gonna take the couch, are you?" The plaintiveness in his voice made her pivot. "The lady in the coffee shop said she don't mind if I sleep on it. She said I could use it as long as I wanted, and she wouldn't call for it to be picked up."

"Sal, you know the rules. Furniture isn't allowed in alleys. Sanitation found the body, so they probably already called bulky-waste pickup."

"Can you do something? I had to fight a couple guys over that couch."

"I'll see what I can do." She walked off.

"You're a cop! You can do what you damn well please!" he yelled.

The words hit her like blows on the back. She felt a pinch of sympathy but quickly stifled it. If you let it, this job would chew you up and spit you out. She couldn't save the world.

"You handled him well," Fin said.

Desi gave him a sharp look. Now he was trying to flatter her. "I know his limits." She started to walk back to the station. Fin fell in beside her.

"He's a street informant and that's it. A DA would never be able to put him on the stand. A defense attorney would chop a crack addict-turned-drunk homeless man who hasn't showered in three months into coleslaw."

"So the woman in the coffee shop followed John Doe out to the alley," Fin said after a moment.

"And then got scared and ran, leaving him to die or already dead."

"Cold. She could've called 911 then booked," Fin said.

"Maybe she had something to do with his death, branding and cuffing."

"If she did, why the hell would he meet with her?"

"Good question."

"You believe Sal when he said he didn't roll him?" Fin said.

"It's a moot point by now. If he did take it, he smoked up the proceeds last night. It's far down the crack junkie chain by now."

"It's possible the woman took his wallet and phone, didn't want him ID'd," Fin said.

"I was watching Sal's eyes. I think he was lying. He took the stuff.

4

Desi's cell phone rang as she reached the curb. She answered. As they waited to cross the street, Fin observed her. She was slim but not skinny under a navy-blue trouser suit.

Plain-faced but she'd probably be attractive with a little makeup on her wide eyes, her auburn hair out of the severe ponytail, and a couple drinks to loosen the tightness that she wore like armor.

She could be a dyke. There were a fair number of them on the force. They stuck together, queen bees in the hive.

Desi clicked off the phone. "That was the HR woman at TeleBank. They have an employee who didn't come to work and meets John Doe's description."

"Rock and roll," Fin said.

"You're driving." She stepped off the curb.

Fin cheered inwardly. The soft pedal had worked. The compliments, the agreeability, the deference to her judgment. He should've used that from the start instead of the muscular approach.

But he'd saved the situation. He was firmly on the investigation. He could deal with Desi Nimmo.

The Blood Room

"So, how long you been in West LA?" McNab asked as they hit Olympic Boulevard in the plain-wrap Crown Victoria assigned to the detective squad.

"Three years."

"Ever think of transferring out?"

"I live in Venice. I've thought about transferring to Pacific Division, then I'd be able to skateboard to work. I hate long commutes."

"Tell me about it. I live in Riverside. Sixty miles each way."

"But you got a big house, right? Isn't that what you wanted?"

"Two-thousand square feet in a treeless subdivision. And you?"

"A nine-hundred-square foot bungalow with a garden the size of a postage stamp. But I have a view of the ocean. That's what I wake up to every day."

"I bet you surf," Fin said.

"You win. And I bet you don't."

"You win. I ski, though."

"House in Big Bear?"

"You're good. A time-share cabin."

She nodded as if she'd heard it before, which she likely had. Cops loved expensive toys. "You have kids to fill up that big house?" she asked.

"I was engaged but my fiancée got cold feet. So now I rent out two bedrooms to local cops. You?"

She shook her head and stared out the window at the Korean-language billboards flashing by as they sped through K-town.

She turned. "What kind of a name is Finbar?"

"Irish. Saint Finbar is the patron of Cork."

"That explains your gift for blarney then."

He grinned. "She jokes, ladies and gentlemen."

She arched her eyebrows. "Who said I was joking?"

He shook his head, still smiling. "You're tough, Nimmo, you are tough."

They entered downtown LA's scrum of skyscrapers that formed the city's legal and financial hub. A movie set had closed off the street they were looking for. A car was attached to a tow truck with a mounted camera directed at the windshield, ready to be pulled along to fake driving, but no actors were around.

"Anyone famous?" Fin asked as they drove around the block.

"Not that I can see. The TeleBank building's right around the corner."

Fin pulled into a red no-parking zone at the curb and parked.

The view from the fifty-first story window in TeleBank's conference room was panoramic. Across the horizon, the San Gabriel Mountains cut a jagged swath of snow-capped peaks glistening under the sun. In the foreground, starbursts of sunlight bounced off plate glass-sided buildings.

"This is better than a postcard," Desi said.

"You okay with me chiming in during the interview?" Fin asked.

She nodded and returned to staring out the window. McNab seemed all right. He was certainly playing the Mr. Nice Guy card. That hard-ass murder cop persona was probably a defense mechanism. He wanted to prove right away that he was no newbie to be pushed around, show his experience. She'd probably be the same way.

She knew she'd been thorny. She hadn't had time for her therapeutic surf that morning or the previous evening because she stayed late to catch up on letters to the parole board, urging them not to release a couple violent assholes she'd put away, and then she'd had the early callout. Without surfing, she'd started the day tied up in a knot.

It occurred to her that now she had a partner, she could hand off some of the ceaseless tide of paperwork and get to ride the waves more often. Maybe Finbar McNab would work out for that, if nothing else.

The door opened. The detectives turned to see a florid-faced man in his late fifties and a woman with a neat, dark bob. They introduced themselves as Ross Kunkel, vice president of legal affairs, and Moira Reed, human resources director.

"Ross is Sterling Parker's supervisor," Moira said.

After exchanging handshakes, they drew up chairs around one end of the large conference table. Moira carefully placed a manila folder in front of her.

"We're really hoping that this isn't Sterling," she said.

"That's what we're here to find out," Fin said.

Moira flipped open the folder and took out a photo, which she slid across the table to the detectives.

"This is his employee ID photo. His garage card is for a Porsche 911."

Desi needed only a glance to see it was John Doe.

"Home address?" Fin asked.

"An apartment on Wilshire Boulevard in Westwood."

She exchanged a look with McNab. The Pen & Ink Café was less than a mile away from that neighborhood.

"I'm very sorry, but the victim appears to be Sterling," Desi said.

Kunkel blanched and raked his hair with his fingers. "Do you have any idea what happened?"

"Sorry, we can't reveal any details at this early stage, but we do need to trace his last movements," Desi said.

Kunkel managed a terse nod.

"When was the last time you saw Sterling?" Fin asked.

"Yesterday. He was at work as normal," Kunkel said. "He didn't come in this morning and never called, which is very unlike him. He calls when he's going to be late, which isn't often. He's usually here early, by seven-thirty, to beat the traffic. I called him at ten, but he didn't pick up. Then Moira said the police had called asking about any employees who hadn't reported for work."

"What can you tell us about him?" Desi said.

"He's a lawyer, joined us six months ago," Kunkel said. "He had excellent references from an investment bank in New York. He easily passed his three-month probationary period. He was very smart, a good team player, worked hard. I wish my whole department was like him."

"Did he have a girlfriend?" Desi asked.

"I don't know much on the personal front. I know he was single, but he was friendlier with a colleague who's more his age. He might know more about that stuff."

"We'd like to ask the colleague a few questions if you don't mind," she said.

Kunkel turned to Moira.

"Shelby Bussowitz."

She pushed back her chair. "I'll get him. The next-of-kin information is in his personnel file. I suppose you'll need that. I made copies so you can take that with you."

"Ms. Reed? If you wouldn't mind, please don't mention anything about Mr. Parker just yet," Desi said.

"Of course," she said.

The detectives opened the file and scanned it. Sterling Parker was twenty-eight years old. He had worked at a law firm in Boston after graduating from Boston University School of Law, and then had moved to an investment bank on Wall Street, where he'd worked in the legal department until his move to Los Angeles.

His parents, Joy and David Parker of Redbank, New Jersey, were listed as his emergency contacts.

"Did Sterling seem ill over the past few days?" Fin asked.

Kunkel's face registered the answer. "Yes, as a matter of fact. He looked pale and fatigued. I caught him leaning against the wall in the bathroom the other day with his eyes closed. He told me he hadn't been sleeping well."

"Did Sterling take any days off from work for a vacation or anything like that recently?" Desi asked.

"No. He hadn't even taken a sick day."

A pudgy, twenty-something guy with copper-colored hair entered the room. The door clicked softly behind him.

"This is Shelby Bussowitz," Kunkel said. "Take a seat, Shelby."

He sat straight in a chair and smoothed his paisley silk tie several times.

Desi leaned forward and focused on his face. "Mr. Bussowitz, I'm sorry to bring some bad news, but a man we believe may be your colleague Sterling Parker was found dead early this morning in an alley near where he lived in West LA."

Shelby blinked several times. It took a moment for him to speak. "Jesus." He gulped.

"I know this is a shock, but I do need to ask you some questions. We're trying to piece together what happened to him last night and in the days leading up to his death," Desi said.

Shelby looked bewildered. "I spoke to him just before nine. I called him because he had some documents I needed to finish a report. I was working on it at home to get it done to meet an East Coast deadline this morning. He was in a rush. He said he was on his way out, and he'd be home in about an hour and send the file then, but he never did."

"Did he say where he was going or if he was meeting someone?"

"No. He said he'd just called an Uber, so he had to get downstairs."

"Why was he taking Uber and not his car?" Fin said.

"He was super careful about his Porsche. He never drove it if he thought he was going to have to park it on the street. I assumed he was going somewhere that involved street parking."

"Was he dating anyone?" Desi asked.

"He said he was taking a break from that. He was going to get engaged back in New York and then she called it off. That's why he moved to LA, to make a fresh start."

Desi leaned forward slightly. "Did you ever notice any odd bruises or marks on Sterling?"

Shelby perked. "Come to think of it, I once saw him sitting at his desk, rubbing some kind of ointment into his wrists. They had black and blue marks on them. As soon as he realized I was standing there, he pulled down his sleeves and threw the ointment into a drawer. He looked really embarrassed. I asked him if everything was all right and he said, 'Yeah, fine,' and changed the subject. It was kind of odd."

Desi exchanged a glance with Fin. "When did you notice those bruises?" she asked.

Shelby thought. "Maybe a month ago, no, more like five or six weeks."

"I think that's all for now," Desi said, grabbing the personnel folder. "You've been very helpful."

The detectives gave them business cards and shuffled out to the lobby to wait for the elevator.

"Sounds like Sterling Parker had an urgent appointment with this woman," Fin said.

"And the meet was set for nine o'clock since Shelby said Parker was rushing when he spoke to him just before nine. The barista said the spilled drink occurred shortly before closing, which was at nine-thirty. The coroner's tech put time of death at roughly eight to ten p.m. It all fits."

The elevator chimed and doors slid open. Desi stepped in and punched the button.

"You know what I'm thinking?" Fin said. "He could have been on a coffee date with someone he met online. That could explain why the woman didn't call 911 or want to get involved. She'd just met him."

The elevator halted.

"But if he was feeling sick, why would he go on a coffee date at all?" Desi said as they exited. "I would've canceled."

"Maybe he was the type who insisted on toughing it out. They said he'd never taken a sick day," Fin said.

"But he was meeting a woman. You're not going to impress a girl if you show up sick on the first date. He had to have been running a fever and in pain. He was in no shape to be flirting," Desi said. "No, Sterling needed to meet that woman for a reason. A reason that was worth sitting on a festering wound."

They reached the car and got in. Fin pulled out of the curb and slid into traffic.

"Maybe he knew this woman," he said.

"I think he did. I think she may have inflicted the injuries at his request."

Fin shot a curious look at her.

"He obviously hadn't sought treatment for the injuries and had been at work every day. He had bruises on his wrists as long ago as six weeks."

"Are you ..." Fin said.

"I think our guy was into hard-core kinky sex, the beat-me-whip-me kind. I think we're looking at a homicide."

5

It was mid-afternoon. Desi and Fin had divvied up footage from two businesses on the block that had surveillance cameras, as well as the street cam from the nearby intersection with a traffic light.

They had spotted Sterling Parker arriving at the café in the Uber and entering by the front door, but not a woman with a long, dark ponytail.

Desi leaned back in her chair. "We've got two witnesses who say she was there. She must've approached from the residential side streets, entered the alley and gone in the café's back door."

"Which means she'd been there before."

"And maybe that she didn't want to be seen."

Desi got up and walked to the break room, where she grabbed a couple granola bars from a box she kept in a cabinet. She opened one and slid the rest into her jacket pockets.

The investigation was ramping up, which meant she'd have little time for meals for at least the next twenty-four hours, maybe more like forty-eight.

She didn't eat much during a major investigation anyway. Caffeine and adrenaline took her appetite, but she knew from experience that if she didn't force herself to eat something, the lack of food would catch up to her with a blinding headache or a dizzy spell later on.

She poured herself her umpteenth mug of coffee and looked up as Keisha Hardy walked in.

"You caught yourself a new partner and a homicide on the same day. That fresh?" Keisha said.

"Just made it." Desi settled against the counter and dipped the granola bar into the coffee. "I got stuck with the new guy because of the homicide. Lieutenant's orders."

"Could be worse." She hiked her eyebrows at Desi. "Single?"

"So he says. You go for it, girl."

"You forget, I'm spoken for," Keisha said.

"It's serious with Pablo, then?"

Keisha stirred sugar into her coffee and tapped the teaspoon on the side.

"He's asked me to move in with him."

"Whoa. And?"

"I just gave my landlord my thirty-day notice."

"Congrats. Another match made in blue heaven." Desi chewed her coffee-soaked granola bar.

"You need to find someone. You've been alone too long, Desi."

"Well, it won't be another cop. You know what they say, once burned ..."

"If we're going to go cliché, here's another one: get back in the saddle."

Desi sighed. "Cops are dogs."

"There're a few who aren't."

"I have yet to find one. You know how it is, civilian guys feel threatened by women cops so we're left with the canines in the pound."

"I've been there, but hey, I found Pablo. You want me to see if he's got any buddies downtown?"

"Thanks, but I'll pass."

"Let me know. Your surfboard doesn't warm your bed at night."

Desi pushed herself off the counter. "I love my board, and it loves me. Best thing, it never talks back."

John Stamos entered. "This coffee klatch only for ladies or can anyone join?"

"Too late, Stamos," Keisha said. "The clock struck midnight. Cinderella is leaving the ball." She left with Desi on her heels.

"Hey, Desi," Stamos called. She turned. He lowered his voice. "You find out why McNab left Newton?"

"Nope, and tell the truth, I'm not that interested."

"Anyone who starts out by saying 'tell the truth' follows with a lie."

"Aren't you the shrink today?" Desi said.

Stamos mock winced. "Touchy, touchy."

"Gotta go. I'm waiting on a warrant."

Desi walked back to her desk. Stamos was right. She *was* interested in why Fin McNab, Mr. Murder Cop, had left the tough, gang-infested Newton area for the relatively tame West LA division. Burnout, as he had intimated, was a possibility, but McNab didn't seem burned out. In fact, he seemed the opposite—raring to go.

While she'd written up the search warrant for Parker's apartment, he'd traced the building through property records, found the building's owner and called the management company to let them know the situation and that they'd be there for a search in a matter of hours.

It was a relief to have someone to do all that, and without being told. She sat at her desk and saw the DA's email she'd been waiting for had arrived. She clicked it. The judge had signed the search warrant.

"Hey, McNab, you ready to toss Parker's crib?"

Fin swiveled in his chair. "Rock and roll."

Yep, the story behind his transfer definitely lay beyond just wanting a change.

Sterling Parker lived on Wilshire Boulevard's winding section known as "condo canyon" for the swank high-rises that flanked both sides of the six-lane thoroughfare slicing through the affluent area of Westwood.

"I definitely chose the wrong career," McNab muttered as he pulled into the horseshoe drive of a building identified by a sign as the Wilshire Arms. He parked in the spot marked "Delivery."

"Justice is a higher calling," Desi said as they got out.

"I don't know. Living in luxury seems like a pretty high calling to me," he said.

A stylishly dressed woman from the property manager's office who identified herself as Belinda Jennings was waiting for them in the lobby.

She snapped a photo of the warrant with her phone and took them and their empty evidence boxes up to the third floor in the elevator.

"Any problems with Mr. Parker as a tenant?" Fin asked her.

"No complaints. He always paid his rent on time. Such a tragedy. He was so young."

The elevator opened. The tang of furniture polish hung in the hallway as they walked to three-o-nine. The woman unlocked the door and Desi thanked her.

The detectives snapped on gloves as they sized up the place. At first glance, nothing indicated it could be a potential crime scene, the place where his injuries had been inflicted. It was a compact, one-bedroom apartment, sparsely furnished with Ikea in young bachelor style.

By the lack of clutter, it looked like he hadn't lived there long. The garish blue light on a wifi modem on the TV stand flickered, breaking the stillness.

"You take the bedroom and bathroom, and I'll take the kitchen and living room?" Desi said.

"Roger."

McNab disappeared down a short hall as Desi took out her phone and snapped a few photos of the living room, extra protection in case of later claims of missing items although there was likely little chance of that since the occupant was dead.

The room was dominated by a large flat-screen TV in front of a couch and coffee table. She picked up a small pile of DVDs on the table. Who had DVDs anymore? She shuffled through them, pausing at each one. They contained the answer that she'd suspected.

The covers depicted women clad in scanty, black leather outfits and wielding whips and chains, men in full-face masks, menacing with maces and nunchucks. The titles matched the scenes: "Dungeon of Hades." "Midnight Soul." "The Blood Room." Porn of the BDSM variety—bondage, domination, sadism and masochism.

"Hey, I found it. Our guy was leading a double life," she called. "What did I tell you?"

"No kidding," McNab called back. "Come check this out."

She scooted into the bedroom where McNab was crouching in front of two office-storage cardboard boxes he'd pulled from the closet.

He picked up a handful of their contents: a coil of rope, handcuffs, a black leather choker studded with metal spikes and a wrestler-style head mask.

"Looks like he was heavy-duty into this shit," McNab said.

"Jesus. He was hard-core," Desi said.

"Well, if he was into being branded ..."

"You find the branding iron?" she asked.

"Not so far."

"Bag and tag all of it," Desi said.

She returned to the living room, depositing the DVDs into an evidence bag and labelling it before moving on to the kitchen. The cupboards were largely bare.

A drawer was full of takeout remnants: soy sauce and ketchup packets, plastic utensils and fast-food napkins.

The fridge revealed more of Parker's single-guy diet: a six-pack of craft beer, a couple yogurts and a restaurant leftover box. A to-do list lay on the counter alongside a pen. She picked it up.

"Eggs, laundry, car wash."

He was organized.

She looked at the table. There was a thick book with a plain hardcover, the type that filled rows of shelves in law offices. "U.S. Immigration Law" was embossed in gold lettering on the front.

What would a corporate lawyer be doing studying federal immigration rules?

She thumbed through it, but he hadn't marked any pages, nor was there anything noted on the legal pad next to it although a jagged top edge showed pages had been torn off.

A laptop sat next to the pad, plugged into the wall. She idly lifted the lid and pressed a random key.

To her surprise, the screen flashed to life. Red and orange flames licked the borders of a black page. A block of text sat in the center.

Desi lowered herself into the chair.

> Thanatos
>
> The dungeon where you can realize your darkest delight. Our mistresses will take you on a journey across the River Styx into the Hades that knows no boundaries.

Thanatos was underscored. Desi clicked it. A new page popped up displaying photos of two women, their faces covered by masks. "Mistress Achlys" had a crow's wing of black, shiny hair and was wearing a type of leather harness and thigh-high boots. She brandished a bent riding crop in both hands as if ready to release one end to make a forceful strike.

The face and hair of the other one, "Mistress Odyne," were obscured by a Venetian-style mask with oversize silver and black feathers. She was dressed in a Catwoman-style suit with cutouts to reveal key anatomical parts. A leather cat-o-nine tails dripped from her hand.

McNab entered the living room. "I'm done."

She swiveled the laptop screen to show him.

He emitted a low whistle. "Just the kind of girls you want to take home to momma."

"We lucked out. It's not password-protected."

"He obviously didn't use it for work then."

"We need to find these women and this place, Thanatos," Desi said.

"One of them could be our mystery woman."

"Possible. Anything in the bathroom?"

He held up an evidence bag containing a half empty bottle of ibuprofen.

"He was probably taking this for the pain. And here's evidence that he was dressing that wound." He held up another bag of used gauze bandages, streaked with blood and pus. "These were in the garbage."

"Lovely." Desi closed the laptop. "I'm going to bag this."

"You wanna try the garage? I bet his Porsche is parked there," Fin said.

"It's on the warrant."

After locking up the apartment, the detectives descended in the elevator with the evidence boxes and stepped out into the garage's dank, musty air. Desi pressed the Porsche fob on Sterling Parker's keychain. A beep sounded from the depths of the concrete cavern.

Their heads turned as they tried to pinpoint the car's location. She pressed the fob again. McNab signaled the far-right corner. Their footsteps echoed as they crossed the floor, passing a fleet of Mercs, BMWs, and Audis.

"That's it," he said, pointing. "Silver Porsche Carrera, next to the red 'Vette."

After gloving up, the cops opened the Porsche's doors. The interior bore a strong new-car smell and not a speck of dust.

"Looks like Bussowitz was right. He treats this car like a baby." Desi slid into the driver's seat.

"I would too, considering what it cost." Fin pulled out a sheaf of documents from the glove compartment and rifled through them. An insurance card and the manufacturer's maintenance manual. He tossed them back in and closed the door.

Desi clicked on her flashlight and checked the visor then the floor. Clean. She shone it down the crevice along the side of the seat. The light caught something yellow. She fished out a piece of lined paper, torn from a legal pad. The one in the apartment?

"Ruslana Ludmila Cojocaru" was carefully printed on it in almost childish capital letters. It wasn't the same handwriting as on the to-do list, which was more than likely written by Sterling Parker. Someone had given him this name.

Desi held out the piece of paper for Fin to examine.

"Ruslana. Sounds like it could be Russian," he said.

Desi shrugged and slid the fragment into a bag, which she deposited in an evidence box.

They checked the trunk and car's exterior but discovered nothing else. Returning upstairs, they found Belinda Jennings talking to a heavily-jowled, older man in the lobby. A strong cooking smell of meat and onions wafted out of an open door behind him.

"We're done," Desi said.

"I was just telling Arkady about Sterling Parker. He's the concierge," Belinda said.

Arkady. A Russian name and he had a wide, flat Slavic face. Desi pulled out the piece of paper from the car and showed it to him.

"Do you know anyone by this name who may have come to the building or maybe works in the apartments?"

He peered at the paper. "No. I don't know," he said in a heavy accent.

"Is it a Russian name?"

"Is not Russian."

"Any idea where it might come from?"

He shook his head.

"Thanks." She said goodbye to both of them and headed to the car.

Fin had already piled the evidence boxes into the Crown Vic's trunk and was sitting behind the wheel.

"It's not a Russian name," she said, closing the door. She filled him in on her brief interview with Arkady.

"Huh. Another mystery woman," Fin said.

"Or maybe the same one," Desi said.

6

Fin negotiated the left turn onto busy Wilshire and nosed into the thick chain of traffic. It was now full-on rush hour.

"What's the deal with people getting their rocks off with whips and chains?" he said. "I could never figure that one out."

"Beats me," Desi said.

He looked at her, smiling.

"Whoa. She's on a roll with the jokes today. They're bad ones, but I'll take them."

She twitched a smile back. "You ever work any cases with an S&M angle?"

"Never. Newton was gang and narcotics beefs, and the usual DV shit, of course."

"I used to work alongside the vice crew in Hollywood, which was pretty active, so I'd hear about it from time to time. The clubs are real careful to stay on the down-low. The last thing they want is cops sniffing around. BDSM isn't illegal, but causing harm to someone, even if they want to be harmed, is," she said.

"I get it. It's one of those grey areas. If there's no complaint, we don't generally go after it since it's between consenting adults," Fin said.

"Exactly, but if someone dies, it's a whole other ball game," Desi said.

Fin stopped at a red light. "Why'd you leave Hollywood? That's a high-profile station. And from what I've seen, you're a good detective."

Desi gazed out the window. "Long story." One she didn't need to spill. She switched the subject.

"I can't help but think that Parker would probably still be alive if he'd gotten medical help."

"It's a helluva thing to die over," Fin said.

They were inching past the veterans' cemetery, caught in the glut of vehicles pouring into the funnel of the 405 freeway onramp.

"There's always the possibility that he was harmed against his will," she said.

"You mean like he was a victim of blackmail or extortion over his lifestyle?"

"Yeah, he wouldn't pay up, so they leaned on him."

"Whatever it was, he died to keep a secret," Fin said. "Wouldn't be the first dumbass to do that." The traffic crawled in the choked lanes. He shifted in his seat. "Goddamn, now I know why everybody hates the Westside, and why you made me drive. You got me back, Nimmo."

"I have my ways," she said.

"This really is a weird homicide," Fin said. His blue eyes were as bright as sun bouncing off snow.

She studied him. He was certainly gung ho. Maybe just a little too much.

They checked the items taken from Sterling Parker's apartment into the evidence room with the exception of the laptop, which Desi signed out to examine, and trooped up to the squad room.

It was past four, the regular bailout time for most detectives, and the room was empty except for one head of raven hair bent over a computer.

"McNab, meet Len Martinez, our midwatch guy. He's worked a lot of vice," Desi said.

Fin detoured over to a desk where a man built like an oak stood and extended a pancake-sized palm. Fin shook it.

"His first day in West LA, and we caught a homicide," Desi said.

"Oh yeah?" Martinez raised eyebrows thick as caterpillars.

She outlined the case so far. "We think the victim's injuries might be linked to this BDSM place called Thanatos," she finished. "You ever heard of it?"

Martinez shook his oversize head.

"Some of those clubs are underground, especially if they're into the real heavy kinky shit. They come and go, move around. I never heard of branding people, but I can't say it doesn't exist. Some of the upscale ones operate strictly on a referral basis—new members can only be referred by a current member. If this guy's a corporate type, he's probably in one of those. He wouldn't risk being recognized at a regular club."

"Thanks, I'll keep you posted," Desi said.

"Let me know if you need a hand." Len resumed his seat, and Desi and Fin crossed to their desks.

She tapped the laptop.

"I'm going to see what else I can find on this website, but that doesn't mean you have to stick around." It was a test. She dangled the last part to give him an out.

"No way. I'm all in. The first twenty-four after a homicide are all or nothing."

"Appreciate it." He wasn't a clock-watcher. That was good. "I need you to help track down this Thanatos place."

"I do have a question though," he said.

"What?" She plugged in the laptop and opened it, holding her breath that the website was still there. It was.

"Do you ever eat?"

"Not a lot when I'm working a case. But you go ahead and grab dinner. There's a bunch of takeout menus on the bulletin board in the break room."

"You want something? I'm buying."

"I won't turn down a free meal."

Fin walked to the break room. "You like Thai?" he called out the door.

"Perfecto."

Fin ordered two kung pao chickens and rice, and they divided up search tasks. When the food arrived, hunger took over. They ate in silence then leaned back.

"I clicked on the dommes' names and a password request came up." Desi swiped her mouth with a napkin.

"Extra security layer."

"Yep, so I can't get much else out of the website. When I called up Thanatos.com on my PC, it brings up a black page with a request for a password, nothing else. I'll have to get our resident geek on it in the morning, see if he can find a back door into the site."

"I got something through the domain name registry." Fin picked up his notepad. "Thanatos.com is registered to Olympus Enterprises. The California Secretary of State business registry lists Olympus Enterprises as active, and Martin Groves as the registered agent in Beverly Hills. He's the only officer listed, which is unusual. I did an internet search on him. He's a CPA and he's still in BH. We can hit him up tomorrow."

"Olympus fits the Greek theme." She called up a webpage. "Check this out. 'Thanatos is the personification of death in Greek mythology." She started reciting. " 'Achlys is the Greek goddess of poisons, or the mist over the eyes that precedes death. May have been a daughter of Nyx or Night. The personification of misery and sadness.' And 'Odyne is the daughter of Nyx and the goddess of Pain, the personification of woe'."

"That's one happy family," Fin said.

"You get anything on that Ruslana name?"

"No hits whatsoever, not even DMV. There can't be too many people with that name."

"Huh. Illegal maybe?"

"I'll check with ICE tomorrow."

"I went through the rest of Parker's laptop, including his personal gmail account, which was open. There was nothing that indicated any meeting last night or anything with the S&M stuff."

"He probably used an encrypted app on his phone," Fin said.

"The autopsy's skedded for tomorrow, eight a.m. I'll go," Desi said. She scraped the last bit of chicken from the cardboard container and chewed it. "That was good. I was hungrier than I thought. Thanks."

"Hey, brains need food."

"You sound like my mom."

"This not-eating thing goes back a ways then."

"Food's never been my thing."

"What has?" His eyes met hers. They were serious.

"Hey, I just met you."

His look lightened.

"Too soon, I get it. *Excusez-moi.*" Fin stretched. "That's about all we can do tonight. Let's get out of here, get some sleep."

"Go ahead. You've got a long drive. I'll check the laptop back into the evidence room."

He didn't waste any time. The sound of his feet rippling down the stairs faded, leaving an empty silence. Desi looked for Len. He was either out on a callout or maybe he'd gone, too. She'd lost track of time.

The squad room took on an eerie quality late at night, as if victims floated out from case files to demand the wrongs against them be put right.

"I'm working on it," she told them in her head. "But I'm just one overloaded, overwhelmed, nearly burnt-out cop."

She shivered. The station turned meat-locker cold with few people around to give off body heat. She rubbed her arms, gathered her jacket, purse and laptop and shuffled downstairs.

The morning watch desk officer was flipping through the pages of a nearly day-old newspaper, his back hunched like an apostrophe over the desk. Every station had a few oddballs who preferred the graveyard shift.

People who didn't much like people, who preferred the freedom from responsibility, who wanted to escape the scrutiny of station brass, quietly collect checks until they put in their twenty-five years and could retire.

They were generally an underappreciated lot and taken for granted. But having them meant others didn't get stuck with the havoc of an upside-down life. Desi had had to endure several stints of working "the late show" as a patrol officer working the Northeast Valley. She had hated every minute of it.

She deposited the laptop in the evidence room, signed the log, and headed out to the parking lot.

The Pacific Ocean had unfurled a thick carpet of fog over the Westside as the temperature dropped. Visibility was just a few feet. She pressed her keyless remote. Her car's taillights bloomed fuzzily in the mist.

If the marine layer was this thick a couple miles from the ocean, it would get worse as she headed west toward Venice. She hit the street and crawled along, hunched over the wheel. Few motorists were out.

It had been a long, eventful, and fitful day. An offbeat homicide, a new partner dumped on her, initial combat turned into a reluctant truce. A wave of exhaustion swept over her.

She pulled into her alley that bordered the rear of the packed blocks of pedestrian-only lanes shoved hard against Venice Beach. Her wooden bungalow was just a couple blocks from the famed boardwalk, which wasn't a boardwalk at all but a ribbon of asphalt hemming a golden sheet of sand.

On weekends, it turned into a free-for-all carnival of freak acts and bongo-banging flower children. During the summer, it became almost unbearable. Thousands of daytrippers converged on Venice to experience the scene, plus bands of roving junkies and meth heads who slept rough and lived off handouts and theft.

Despite the nuisances, Desi stayed. She couldn't live without the ocean. It was how she survived the job—and life.

She parked in the garage and headed through the tiny back garden to the back door. Entering the kitchen, she flung her purse on the table and flipped the switch on her electric kettle to make chamomile tea with the deftness formed of habit.

As the water heated, she passed through the living room where her surfboard stood next to the front door, ready to ride.

It wasn't much of a companion, as Keisha had pointed out. Maybe she should get a dog. She'd long debated getting one, but it wouldn't be fair to the animal with the hours she worked. A cat would be better. They were more independent, didn't need walking or washing.

She opened the front door and fished in the mailbox on the wall next to it for the day's post. Junk mail and the latest issue of The Gold Shield, the monthly newsletter of the LAPD detectives' union. She switched on the TV to fill the silence and went to the bedroom to change into pajamas.

On her way back to the kitchen, she picked up the newsletter and skimmed the headlines as she poured the boiling water into the mug.

A grievance had been filed over stricter requirements for reporting personal finances to the department. Familial DNA searches were becoming standard practice. A lawsuit had been filed against the department by the parents of a girl killed by an off-duty detective during a pursuit of a suspect in a residential area. That had been a horrific case that had caused a huge ruckus in the community and in the department.

A photo on the bottom of the front page caught her eye.

A quiver spread through her body, jogging her hand holding the kettle. Water poured onto the counter. Shit. She set down the kettle before she burned herself.

7

The photo showed Rondell Nichols, beaming as he and a captain held a cheesy-looking plaque between them. "Nichols named Hollywood Detective of the Year," the headline declared.

He'd beamed those Chiclet teeth at her once as they lay wrapped in the afterglow, and she'd slipped into that smile, right past the wedding ring on his finger.

Six months later, after his wife had shown up at the station demanding to see her rival, the captain called Desi into his office and hit her with Rondell's sucker punch. He'd filed a sexual harassment complaint against her.

He had unmoored her from the dock of his promises, abandoning her to drift alone while remaining in the safe harbor of his marriage and in doing so, deep-sixed her career.

Her lawyer worked out a settlement after threatening to file a countercomplaint. The complaint would be quietly dropped if she simply transferred out of Hollywood, which she had loved. West LA needed a detective so that was where she'd landed, in a curled up ball that she hadn't allowed to unfurl.

She looked closer at Nichols' hand holding the plaque. A hint of gold flashed on his ring finger. Still married, and he was still winning. She felt the old wound tearing apart her chest.

She ripped the newsletter in half, then again and again until the shreds spilled from her hands. She flung the pieces into the sink, grabbed a book of matches from a drawer and tossed a lit match to them. As she watched the flame curl his grin into a brittle char, she regained her sense of calm.

Finbar McNab careened off the freeway into suburban strip of shopping centers and big box stores, the emptiness of their parking lots illuminated under the sulfurous white haze of towering light poles.

He reached the turnoff for his cookie-cutter development of ranch homes roofed with dull red Spanish tiles and sped through the silent streets with improbable names for a desert town—Oak, Maple, Birch, Sycamore. Finally, Willow Avenue and his driveway.

The pickup truck and SUV parked outside told him his housemates were home. They were likely several beers into the night, watching a sports channel. He didn't feel like dealing with them.

He heaved himself out of his car, feeling the return of burden, the ache in his life. He should sell the house and move closer to LA. Even with the rent money from the housemates, the mortgage and taxes ate his paycheck. He could be paying the same amount of money to live in the city, maybe even less accounting for the cost of his commute. At least he'd have a life.

The big house in the suburbs had been Ginger's idea. And he'd wanted to give her everything she wanted, including the emerald-cut, one-carat diamond ring with a platinum halo band, which she hadn't bothered to return. Shallow, according to his mother, and exceedingly bad form. She'd never liked Ginger.

Unfortunately, he hadn't found out about Ginger's shallowness before that expensive purchase but as Mom said, just as well he'd found out. Still, the revelation had come at a price that he wasn't sure had been worth paying. After Ginger had left, his whole life had slipped sideways. Now look where he'd landed.

The house was ablaze with lights. Feeling a tweak of annoyance, Fin flicked them off as he passed through the kitchen into the den where, as he'd predicted, Ron and Jesus were lolling on opposite ends of the L-shaped sectional sofa watching the Lakers, Heineken cans lined up like soldiers on the coffee table.

"Hi, honey, how was your day?" Ron squeaked in a falsetto.

"Getting in that OT, Nabster?" Jesus said.

"Remember to turn off the lights." Fin headed upstairs to his palatial master bedroom suite.

"Lakers are winning," Jesus called.

"Great," he replied flatly from the stairs.

Who cared? Fin closed the door, shutting out the TV cheers and chatter. He shucked off his shoes and flung them across the field of beige plush-pile carpet. The king-sized bed stared at him, a vast empty plain. Another of Ginger's must-haves.

She had insisted on the king-size mattress because she said he was like an elephant when he turned.

He looked at the portrait that he'd painted of her leaning against the wall in front of the bed. He'd once congratulated himself for painting her wide brown eyes so true-to-life. Now he cursed their realism.

They seemed to follow him wherever he went in the room. Still, he couldn't find it in himself to remove the painting or even turn it to face the wall. It seemed as integral to the room as the walk-in closet. He knew he was torturing himself, but after what had happened in Newton, he deserved it.

He entered the en suite bathroom with the his-and-hers sinks and towel racks. As he brushed his teeth, he remembered there was still hope. His first day in West LA and he'd caught a murder, and it was looking like it had the earmarks of a high profile case.

Maybe his luck had finally turned, and this "punishment" would work out. If he could clear this homicide, everybody would be sorry they'd ever discounted Fin McNab. Including Ginger. Especially Ginger.

The Los Angeles County Department of the Coroner was located east of downtown along a road of grubby auto repair and parts places, most with signs in Spanish. When compared with the high-rent, mostly white Westside, Desi thought, this was a whole different city.

She drained the second of her two large lattes, which she had desperately needed. It had been a fitful night of sleep due to the re-entry of Rondell Nichols into her consciousness. Seeing that photo had awakened a raft of feelings that she thought she'd erased but really were just lying dormant.

Hatred, anger, resentment, and yes, bitterness. She hurled the cup in the trash at the foot of the steps into the building and jogged up. She had to bury it all, yet again.

She threaded her arms through her jacket sleeves and buttoned up. The morgue's inner chambers were kept at a frosty forty-five degrees.

Somber Black and Latino faces filled the waiting room on the left, minorities being overrepresented in untimely deaths in L.A. County. A young woman, her shoulders caped in a sheet of hair, sobbed on the shoulder of a man wearing a battered straw cowboy hat.

On the right was a gift shop that sold death-themed knick-knacks such as beach towels and mugs printed with body outlines. Desi had one of those mugs somewhere. Homicide detectives were the shop's biggest customers.

An acrid chemical odor pinched her nostrils as she headed deeper into the building. The alternative smell, though, would be a lot worse. She garbed up in the disposable scrubs and headed into the autopsy room where Sterling Parker awaited the knife like a marble statue poised under the sculptor's chisel.

Despite his waxy death mask, she could see he'd been handsome. Smooth, even features. Straight nose, thick hair with a wave in it. A lean trim physique.

Dr. Amita Rajput, the forensic pathologist, entered, peering over her bifocals at Desi.

"Detective Nimmo, you're interested in this case?" She was a native of Mumbai, and her cadence carried both a British inflection and a singsong lilt.

"I am. It's an odd one."

"We shall see what he has to tell us. Dead men do not lie." It was her standard line.

A microphone was lowered on a cable from the ceiling to record the pathologist's observations, and she started talking through her visual examination of the corpse, scrutinizing his skin, paying special attention to the tips of his fingers, the veins in his arms and feet.

She peered at his nostrils and mouth and took swabs. "No outward evidence of drug use or puncture marks indicating hypodermic use," she pronounced.

She honed in on the bruising on the ankles and wrists. "The contusions are consistent with tight handcuffs or restraints, probably five to seven days preceding death," she said.

The techs turned the body. The nasty wound on Parker's buttock immediately drew her attention. "What have we here?" she murmured, grabbing a magnifying glass.

She raised her voice as she examined it. "A mark in the shape of an oval with a horizontal line across the center, located on the lateral of the left buttock."

She took a ruler and measured it.

"Three inches high by two and one quarter wide. The mark appears to be a third-degree burn and to have subsequently been infected. By the advanced state of the infection, possibly eight to ten days ago. Red streaks indicate sepsis is present.

"The rear of the subject's thighs shows latter-stage contusions on each leg consistent with blunt force trauma from a large, flat instrument, also probably eight to ten days ago."

Desi hadn't seen the thigh bruising before. Was there any part of the guy that hadn't been bashed? Could this really all have been voluntarily inflicted?

Dr. Rajput's eyes travelled upward. "Subject's upper and middle back display red circular marks, second-degree burns consistent with the size of a cigarette end but some are larger in dimension, perhaps consistent with the size of a cigar."

She measured the circumference of the spots and counted them. "There are twenty-one such marks in total, eleven small, ten large. It looks they were inflicted on two separate occasions. The smaller ones I would say about three weeks ago, the larger ones about eight days ago. The upper back has nine horizontal welts where the skin was broken. State of healing indicates they were inflicted possibly several months ago."

The pictures on the Thanatos website. The dommes holding whips and riding crops.

Desi's cell phone rang just as the body was turned again on its back so Dr. Rajput could slice along the right clavicle, starting the Y-shaped incision that would peel the torso open for the internal exam.

Making an apologetic face to Dr. Rajput's frown of censure, she fumbled for the phone in her pocket and pushed through the swinging doors to the hallway. Just as well. She didn't need to witness the examination of organs. She wasn't squeamish but it wasn't her favorite scene.

It was McNab. "Hey, I'm at the station. Sterling Parker's parents just called. They just got into LAX and want to talk to us. I told them to come to the station. You want me to handle?" he said.

"The autopsy's not done, but I'll see what I can get out of Rajput now. Give them coffee. I'll be there in an hour."

"Roger. I put a call into ICE on that Ruslana name. I should hear back soon."

After clicking off, Desi scrolled through the Times website. There was no mention of a body found in West LA. That was good. Media coverage tended to amp up the pressure for a quick solve both from downtown and divisional brass.

She returned to the autopsy room, where a tech was jumbling several feet of intestines into the abdominal cavity, and another was closing flaps of the scalp with Frankenstein sutures.

"Doc, I gotta head out. Any verdict so far?"

She looked up. "Brain abscess, caused by a bacterial infection entering his bloodstream from the infected wound on the buttock. He died of sepsis. I will order a blood culture, so we know exactly what type of bacteria it was."

"Any sign of sexual activity before death?"

"No fluids in the usual spots," she answered with a tad of annoyance. "Now I really must finish up here. Although the dead are a patient lot, the living are not, and they are the ones I ultimately have to answer to."

"Doctor, I am most grateful," Desi said formally. "So just to confirm, we're talking homicide?"

"It is highly likely that someone inflicted the burn wound so that's unless I find some evidence to the contrary, that's going to be my ruling."

8

Fin McNab stood and hitched his trousers. He was about to go downstairs to tell Joy and David Parker to grab breakfast at the café across the street when he spotted Lt. Butler unlocking the door to her office. He sat back down, pretended to busy himself and waited, keeping an eye on Butler's door. A minute later, she crossed to the break room. He grabbed his coffee mug and followed.

"Morning LT," he said. "How's it going?"

She glanced up from replacing the carafe on the hot plate. "Better now that I'm out of that meeting downtown. Anything new on that body?"

"Nimmo's at the autopsy. The vic's parents are downstairs. They just flew in on a red-eye from the East Coast. They're pretty broken up."

"I don't blame them."

Keisha Hardy walked in holding a lunch bag.

"Morning," she said.

Fin raised his mug at her in greeting as she opened the fridge door and deposited her bag. Damn, now he wasn't going to be able to casually mention that Nimmo wanted him to wait for her to talk to the parents, but he didn't think that was right, making them sit there until she arrived, and maybe then Butler would send him down to talk to them himself.

Butler turned to Keisha. "Come talk to me about that sex assault in the shopping center parking lot. We got a request for a detective to go talk to employees. Keep me posted, McNab." She left.

"Well, I better get to it," he said.

He returned to his desk, sat in his chair and sipped his coffee. Desi could easily be a couple hours in LA traffic. The coroner's department was well east of downtown. Fuck it. He wasn't going to wait for her.

He proceeded downstairs. Joy and David Parker were sitting in the hard plastic chairs along the wall under a bulletin board of wanted posters, roller bags standing next to them. They looked pale and haggard. Fin introduced himself and expressed his condolences.

"Sterling's boss called us. He gave us your name. We thought we'd stop by and see what you've found out," David Parker said. "We want to find out what happened to our son."

"My partner is at the autopsy now, so we'll know more in a little while," he said.

"Autopsy?" Joy's eyes grew large. Her husband placed a cautionary hand on her forearm.

"It's standard procedure in cases of sudden deaths. Shall we go upstairs?"

Joy and David Parker followed Fin to an interview room on the second floor. He offered them coffee, which they declined but accepted water. He brought them paper cups.

"Can you tell us what happened to him?" David Parker said as Fin scraped back a chair to sit across from the couple.

"That's what we're investigating."

Joy Parker's eyes glistened. Fin noted her resemblance to her son across her eyes and nose.

"It's not supposed to happen like this," she said. "Parents aren't supposed to bury children. I wish he hadn't come out here. I

The Blood Room

wish he'd stayed close. If Shay hadn't broken the engagement," she said. A tear trickled down her cheek. Her husband hooked his arm around her shoulders.

"I know this is a very difficult time, but I do need to ask you some questions about Sterling's lifestyle. They might be a little uncomfortable," Fin said, wondering how he was going bring up their son's sexual proclivities.

"Yes, of course," David Parker said. "It's just been a long night. We haven't slept."

"When was the last time either of you spoke to Sterling?" Fin said.

"A couple days ago." Joy sniffed back tears. "He wasn't feeling well. He said he felt weak and feverish. I told him to stay home and rest for a day or two, but he wouldn't. He said he didn't want to draw attention to himself since he was the new hire, and he had a lot of work going on."

"Did he say why he felt sick?" Fin said.

"He said he must've picked up a bug over the past weekend when he was out and about, that it would probably pass."

"He didn't mention a wound or a burn or anything like that?"

They shook their heads. Fin drew the brand mark on his note pad and showed it to them.

"Does this symbol mean anything to you? Have you ever seen it?"

They shook their heads. "No idea," David Parker said.

Fin drew a deep breath. There was no other way to say it than to just come out with it. "We believe Sterling may have been involved with a sadism and masochism sexual lifestyle. He had an infected wound in this shape. He may have been branded as part of the activities at a club he belonged to."

Joy Parker stared in shock.

"Branded?"

Her husband blanched. "That's ridiculous! Sterling would never have gotten involved in something like that."

"He was into helping people," Joy said. "He spent his Saturdays working pro bono at the Legal Aid Society—helping poor people on eviction cases and things like that. It doesn't sound like him at all. Somebody did this to him."

David Parker nodded.

"This has to be some kind of setup."

"We're looking into all angles, Mr. Parker, including the possibility that this was done to Sterling against his will," Fin said. "But whether he consented to it or not, it's a crime and we're investigating this as a homicide."

Joy Parker slumped against her husband. "Homicide?"

"We have witnesses who say they saw a woman with Sterling right before his death. Did he ever mention a girlfriend or a particular female friend?" Fin asked.

"No, he was still getting over Shay." David Parker gave his wife an inquiring look.

She shook her head. "Never mentioned anyone to me."

"Is Shay his former fiancée?" Fin said. They nodded. "I may need to speak to her. Do you have a phone number for her?"

David Parker fished out his phone, scrolled through it and showed the detective the screen. "Shay Stern" and a New York City phone number. "She knows. We called her yesterday," he said. "They were together three years. Met on some online dating thing and hit it off. She's a librarian at the New York Public Library. Nice girl."

Fin wondered what type of dating website they'd met on. "I know this has been a terrible shock. I suggest you go to your hotel and rest up. I'll be in touch as soon as I learn anything."

He handed them business cards and ushered them to the front entrance where they called an Uber.

When he returned, Desi was at the logbook, signing the Crown Vic in. "Ready for the parents?" she said.

Fin's face twisted. "They just left. They couldn't wait so I handled," he said.

Desi looked taken aback. "I got here as fast as I could. You couldn't hold them?"

He shrugged. "They were exhausted after their flight. They just wanted to get it over and done with."

"Oh. Well, what did they say?" Desi said as she walked to her desk, Fin trailing her.

"They said they knew nothing about their son being into S&M. In fact, they said he was just the opposite. He did pro bono work for the Legal Aid Society. They also mentioned his ex-fiancée, Shay Stern, a librarian."

"She should know about Sterling's sexual habits," Desi said. "You get a number?"

Fin waved his black notebook in the air.

"I think I should call her," she said. "Woman to woman and all that."

"Have at it."

He flipped open the notebook and rifled through the pages until he found it. He displayed the page, and she copied the number onto a pad on her desk. "What happened with the autopsy?" he asked.

"Rajput confirmed homicide, cause of death was a brain abscess caused by sepsis from the infected burn wound on his buttock. Speaking of which, we need to check out where someone can get a branding iron made. There can't be too many places."

"You can order them online." Diego Jauregui, the auto theft detective who sat across from Desi, leaned back in his chair and laced his hands behind his head.

"My sister's brother-in-law got one for Father's Day a couple years ago. It has his initials on it so he can brand his steaks on the barbecue. Kind of a gimmicky thing, if you ask me, but he's the kind of guy who has everything."

"I'll check that out," Fin offered.

As Desi settled into her desk, he twisted to his computer and searched "branding iron." Websites offering custom-made branding irons with initials popped up.

"Make grilling your signature dish!" urged one. The sites also sold propane torches to heat the brands with, as well as electric brands.

"Looks like people use them to stamp leather and woodwork, as well as meat," Fin reported.

Desi got up and peered over his shoulder at the screen. "They're too small. Parker's wound was bigger. There must be places that do heavy duty branding irons for ranchers."

He searched branding.

"Says here that branding can be done with hot irons, acid or freezing," he said as he studied a website. "It's not done on livestock as much as it used to because of pressure from animal rights groups. They use microchipping, ear tattoos, and tags instead."

He searched for rancher branding irons and found two places in Texas and one in Wyoming. He called all of them and described the brand he was seeking. They all promised to look in their files.

After hanging up from the last one, he looked around. Desi was hanging up her phone. "I left a voicemail for Shay Stern. Let's pay a visit to Martin Groves in Beverly Hills and see what he can tell us about Thanatos," she said.

The detectives strolled down Rodeo Drive, past the glitzy stores of luxury brands. Japanese tourists, laden with shopping bags, snapped selfies in front of Tiffany's. A passel of Arab women, anonymous in their flowing black hejabs, slipped out of a chauffeur-driven Bentley and streamed into the Chanel boutique. A strip of impeccably manicured, color-coordinated pansies ran along the spine of the street.

"You ever think of lateraling over to Beverly Hills?" Fin asked.

"Who hasn't? They pay the best of any PD in the county," Desi said. "You?"

"Not enough action for me," Fin said.

"Which raises the question why you're in West LA from Newton." Desi drilled him with her eyes.

"Here's the street," Fin said quickly.

They turned off Rodeo and looked for the number of Martin Groves' office.

"This is it."

Fin pointed to a shiny brass plaque on the wall by the door amid a vertical list of similar shingles for lawyers, therapists, and wealth managers. "Martin Groves, CPA."

"You play good cop," Desi said as she pulled open the door.

Groves' office was on the right of a narrow staircase off the first landing. Desi opened the door to a cherry-paneled sanctum. A middle-aged man dressed like a twenty-something in an untucked shirt hovered over a young receptionist's shoulder. He straightened hastily as the detectives entered.

"Martin Groves?" Desi asked.

"Yes?" His hair was too reddish-brown at the temples. Men's dye jobs always showed, Desi thought.

"Detective Desi Nimmo, LAPD."

"Detective Finbar McNab. We need to ask you a couple questions in connection with an investigation."

He looked surprised as they displayed their IDs. "This is a first. You'd better come in then."

The detectives followed him into his office, where he parked himself behind a heavy wooden desk. Fin and Desi took velveteen-upholstered chairs in front of it.

Groves rested his left ankle on his right knee and his hands on the chair arms. He wore no socks under his tasseled loafers. "What can I help you with?" he said, swiveling slightly back and forth in his chair.

He was nervous, Desi thought.

"Are you the registered agent for an entertainment company called Olympus Enterprises?" Fin said.

"Yes," Groves said.

Desi's eyes wandered as Fin talked. The walls were decorated with small Impressionist-style paintings in gilt frames with little lights attached to them, like museum pieces. Maybe they were museum quality. Groves appeared to be doing quite well.

"What type of entertainment does Olympus do exactly?" Fin said.

Groves scratched the underside of his chin and cast his eyes upward. "I don't recall offhand. I'd have to look it up. I'm the registered agent for a lot of small companies." He smiled in a faux apology.

Desi leaned forward.

"Mr. Groves, we can do this the easy way, here, or the hard way, down at the station. It really doesn't matter to us."

Uncertainty—or was it fear?—danced across his hazel eyes. She had rattled him.

"I do have confidentiality to my clients," he said, a hint of defensiveness in his voice.

"Olympus has come up indirectly in our investigation," Fin said. "That's all we can say. It may not be the Olympus we're looking for. There are several companies with that name. We're obligated to check them all out. The sooner we can eliminate this one from our list, the sooner we can be on our way."

Groves looked somewhat relieved. "I suppose if I refuse to tell you, you'll threaten me with a court order or is that just on TV?"

"Some things in TV shows are true, Mr. Groves," Desi said.

"Olympus is an adult entertainment company," he said, addressing Fin.

"Now that your memory's improved, who's the owner?" Desi said.

He hesitated then spoke. "Rory Biesu."

"What can you tell us about Mr. Biesu?" Fin said.

"He's an entrepreneur, a very successful one. He lives in Holmby Hills, works out of his home."

"I'll need that address and phone number," Fin said. "Please."

Groves typed something on his computer, jotted on a notepad then tore off a sheet and gave it to Fin.

"Are you a member of Thanatos, Mr. Groves?" Desi asked.

He paled and quickly lowered the foot that had been resting on his knee, but not before Desi caught sight of a bracelet of odd red marks around his ankle and winding up his shin.

"No, I'm not a member," Martin Groves said.

Desi was sure that was a lie. "But you know what Thanatos is?"

"I've seen it on Mr. Biesu's account sheets."

"Of course, you have. One last thing, do you know anyone named Sterling Parker?"

No recognition registered in his face. He shook his head.

"If there's anything else, we'll be in touch," Fin said.

"I like your art collection, Mr. Groves," Desi said. "The registered agent business must be a good one."

He shrugged. "It has its up and downs." As he got up to escort them to the door, dark scallops showed in the armpits of his sleeves.

"What do you think?" Fin asked once they had gained the sidewalk.

"I think he's calling Biesu right now. Let's get over there. It's not far from here. I'll drive this time," Desi said.

Fin tossed her the keys.

He made a phone call to run Biesu's name as Desi drove along Sunset Boulevard to Holmby Hills, a corner of LA's "golden triangle" of real estate, the other corners being Bel-Air and Beverly Hills.

Phone pressed to his ear, Fin scribbled in his pad, then clicked off.

"Don't tell me, our guy's got a past," Desi said.

"Hell yeah. He's sixty-three YOA with a forty-three-year-old conviction for pandering and a thirty-two-year-old conviction for sex with a minor. Served time on the latter. After that, he's stayed clean."

"So he's a pimp who turned to the legal sex business, or quasi legal, in any case," Desi said.

"Just a regular nice guy," Fin said.

Desi turned off Sunset at the corner where a woman sold maps to movie-star homes from a beach chair with an umbrella. The road wound around the curving leafy streets where the rooftops of palatial mansions poked above ten-foot walls.

"How much do you think the average home costs here?" Fin asked. "Ten, fifteen million?"

"That's probably on the cheap side. That's the Playboy mansion right over there."

Desi pointed to a gate with a long driveway. The house was shielded by a heavy canopy of foliage.

"I'd like to check out that grotto. You ever been on a callout here?" Fin asked.

"No, went to a few domestics in Bel-Air, but that's a slum compared to Holmby. Fifteen million will buy the garage here. There it may get you the whole guesthouse." She braked. "Shit."

An open-top van with "Tours of the Stars" bannered across its sides putted ahead of them as the microphone-wearing driver regaled his passengers with tales of who lived where, although none of the homes were visible. Desi twisted the steering wheel and zoomed around the crawling van. She noted that Fin clutched the ceiling handle as she overtook the vehicle and locked his eyes straight ahead. As she slowed, he relaxed. It was a curious reaction.

She focused on finding Biesu's address. Most of the homes had no numbers on gates and walls so she had to slow to check the curbs where the house numbers were painted. She found Biesu's. Similar to his Holmby Hills neighbors, the property was screened by a massive hedge and a solid metal gate.

Desi pulled into the foot of the driveway where an intercom sat on a metal post at car-window height. A security camera mounted on the gate spied them. She pressed the call button and waited. No answer. She pressed again, this time holding it for three full seconds.

It worked. A woman answered.

"This is the LAPD, Detectives McNab and Nimmo. We need to speak with Rory Biesu." Silence blossomed. "Hello?" Desi said, hiking her eyebrows at Fin.

The voice suddenly returned. "Mr. Biesu's unavailable right now. Can I help you? I'm his assistant."

"We need to ask Mr. Biesu some questions in connection with an investigation. It's just routine."

Another long pause.

The detectives exchanged another look. "He's there," Fin mouthed. Desi nodded.

The assistant returned. "What kind of investigation?" she said.

"I can't divulge that. But if he's not available now, he'll have to come down to the station."

Another pause, then the gate swung slowly open. Desi motored through.

"Biesu was probably standing at her elbow, telling her what to say," Fin said.

"Agreed."

The long driveway ended in a gravel circle in front of a picturesque, Tudor-style stone manse with mullioned windows on the ground floor and gables on the second. Desi parked in front of the entrance and the detectives got out, their footsteps crunching as they walked to the door.

A man with a shock of snowy hair and wearing a burgundy cardigan appeared on the porch, hands peaking the pockets of his slacks.

"I'm Rory Biesu. What can I do for you?" He had a slight accent, hard to place where from.

The detectives flashed their badges.

"We won't take much of your time. We need to ask you some questions. It's just routine, to eliminate lines of inquiry," Fin said.

Biesu frowned.

"We're investigating a homicide, Mr. Biesu," Desi said.

Biesu eyed them for a moment, weighing whether to talk. Curiosity won, or perhaps the desire to prove he had nothing to hide. "Let's go into my study," he said.

They entered a light-filled foyer under a large chandelier. Rainbows shimmied on the walls from sunrays refracted by the crystal prisms.

Biesu led the detectives into a room off the hall. It was lined with stuffed bookshelves. A Persian rug lay on the floor in front of a large fireplace. Next to it stood a rack of long-handled fire tools. Desi sauntered over to it. A brush, a poker, a spade. No brand.

Above the mantelpiece protruded the mounted head of a stag, the large beads of its eyes staring blankly.

The detectives perched themselves on leather wingback chairs in a seating area at one end of the room. Something about the scene nagged Desi as familiar but she couldn't pinpoint it. She nodded at Fin to start the questioning.

"Mr. Biesu, a website registered to your company Olympus Enterprises has come up in the course of an investigation—Thanatos.com. What is the nature of that website?"

He was following the interview playbook. Start with questions the cops knew the answer to in order to gauge the subject's truthfulness.

"It's a private social club."

"What is its purpose specifically?"

Biesu waved his hand in the air. "Socializing, what else."

"BDSM sex?"

"It is all perfectly legal."

Desi took out her phone, punched up Parker's photo and showed it to Biesu.

"Do you know this man?"

She watched Biesu's reaction.

He darted forward and backward as if on a string, barely glancing at it. "No."

"Is he a member of your club?" Desi said.

He shrugged. "I don't know each and every person."

"So he could be a member?"

"I don't run the club."

"Can we talk to the employee who runs the club?"

"She's not here."

"What's her name?"

"My employees, like my clients, have a right to privacy."

Desi was getting annoyed at his evasiveness. She glanced at Fin.

"Where are you from, Mr. Biesu?" Fin asked.

"Romania. I am an American citizen."

"Is adult entertainment your only business?"

"I'm an investor. It's paid off. Let me ask you a question. Why do you think Thanatos has anything to do with this man?"

"We can't say at this time," Desi said.

"Of course not." He stood up. "Is that all? I have told you I don't know the man in the picture. That's what you came here for, no? I have work to do."

The detectives had no choice but to leave. The front door closed with a resounding bang behind them. They crunched back to the plain wrap.

"A regular Mr. Rogers in his cardigan," Fin muttered.

As they motored down the driveway, the gate swung open, and they drove through. A Mercedes SUV bounced to a halt into the next-door driveway. The driver, a woman with a large over-red hairdo and Sofia Loren sunglasses, waited for her gate to creak open.

"Hold on," Desi said. She threw the car into park, bolted out of the car and bounded over the grass strip separating the driveways, waving at the woman with one hand as she pulled out her ID with the other.

The SUV edged forward, then braked as the driver saw Desi. She rolled down the window. Desi shoved her badge in the open space and announced herself. "Do you live here?"

"Yes." Her forehead crinkled in curiosity.

"I'd like to ask you a couple questions about your neighbor, Rory Biesu."

"I don't know what I can tell you. I rarely see him."

"Ever see anything unusual going on over there?"

"He has a lot of traffic in and out of his house."

"What do you mean?"

"He hosts a lot of parties. He's some kind of sleazy Eastern European pornographer who made a fortune in cryptocurrencies. We don't have much to do with him, nor does anyone else on the street."

That better explained how Biesu could afford a Holmby Hills lifestyle. "Cryptocurrencies—like Bitcoin?"

She leaned into the window confidentially. "Well, he told Jerry, my husband, that Bitcoin was old hat already. He suggested we invest in these emerging currencies that are going to be bigger than Bitcoin. He'd made a lot of money with it. He mentioned one to Jerry, what was it?" She paused to think.

Desi was on the verge of saying it didn't really matter when she blurted a name. "Monero, that's it. Jerry told him he'd look into it, but my husband isn't one for taking risks."

"What kind of parties does Biesu throw?"

"Actually, they're generally quiet ones, usually on a Saturday night. We're not on the invite list. Listen, I don't want to be named in some report."

"This is just for informational purposes, but I do need your name."

"Cara Franceschi. Is he in some kind of trouble?"

"No, but keep this to yourself, please. It's a police investigation."

Desi took her phone number and handed her a business card.

"Jerry's going to love this," Cara Franceschi crowed. Her car purred into her estate.

Desi jogged over to Fin, who had pulled the car out of Biesu's driveway and was waiting at the curb. She flung herself in the passenger's seat.

"She say anything useful?" Fin said as he pulled out into the street.

Desi summed up what Cara Franceschi had just told her.

"Which proves ..."

"That he's a total slime bucket who knows a hell of a lot more than he's letting on," Desi said.

Fin pulled away from the curb. "I was surprised Biesu let us in the door."

"He wanted to see what we had on him, if there was more than what we told Martin Groves."

"That was probably our last chance at him. He's undoubtedly lawyering up as we speak," Fin said.

"I'd put money on it. What if these parties are Thanatos?"

"I was thinking the same thing," Fin said.

"We need to get a warrant on that place, but so far we have nothing linking Sterling Parker's death to Biesu, except that the

Thanatos website was on his laptop and Thanatos is one of Biesu's businesses," Desi said.

"Yeah, but we got fatal injuries consistent with rough sex and that's Thanatos," Fin said.

"That might be enough, but we need watertight probable cause. Biesu is going to have some high-priced legal bulldog at his beck and call. That's what you have to deal with in West Latte."

9

Traffic around the Westwood campus of UCLA, bustling with backpacked students, was fluid for once, and they arrived at the station in ten minutes. As she walked across the parking lot, Desi remembered the nagging feeling she'd had in Biesu's study.

"I'll meet you up in the squad room in a minute," she said as they entered the building.

She buzzed downstairs to the property room and asked the officer on duty for the evidence from the Parker apartment search. He disappeared among shelving stacks and returned with a cardboard box.

She fished out the laptop and the bag containing the DVDs, signed the evidence log and exited into the hall.

She couldn't wait until she got upstairs. She paused and looked at the DVD covers through the plastic bag. There it was, in the background of the cover of "The Blood Room," behind a man wearing nothing but a wrestler's full-face mask and red, orange, and yellow flames painted around his groin.

He was holding a white-hot poker and standing on an Oriental rug in front of a blazing fireplace. A nude woman lay supine at his feet with a black executioner's hood over her head.

She ascended the staircase to the squad room two steps at a time, and crossed to Fin's desk, showing him the DVD cover.

"Recognize this?" she said.

Fin did a double take. "Whoa. Talk about full frontal. Are those flames painted on or ... tattooed?" He scrutinized the cover photo.

"Not the guy. Behind him."

Fin studied the cover. "Biesu's fireplace."

"And look what the guy's holding. It implies that he's going to burn someone."

The buzz of Desi's cell phone startled her. A New York area code. Raising her eyebrows at Fin to signal she had something, she sat at her desk and answered. "Detective Desi Nimmo."

"This is Shay Stern. You called me about Sterling Parker?" She spoke in a young woman's clear bell-like pitch.

"I'm very sorry to be calling you at a time like this, but we're conducting an investigation into Mr. Parker's death. Any information you can provide would be helpful."

"Okay."

"I'll get right to the point. I know this is a sensitive issue, but did Sterling have any unusual sexual habits?"

Shay expelled a deep breath.

"He was into masochism. I assume that's what you're referring to."

"He liked being hurt?"

"Yes. He got into some really dark stuff. It was too much for me. That's why I broke up with him. He was always pushing me to go further than I was comfortable with. I'm vanilla now. I left all that behind. I really don't even like talking about it. Did this have something to do with his death?"

"All I can say is that we're looking into everything. This is a big help. When you say, 'Really dark stuff,' what kind of things?"

"Being tied up and put in a box like a coffin. He once attached electrodes to his nipples and had electric shocks. It really started to weird me out."

"What about being burned with cigarettes?"

"Yes."

"Was he ever branded, as in burned with a piece of hot metal?"

"He never said anything along those lines to me, but that sounds like him. He always wanted to go to extremes, pushing himself to go to the brink to see how much pain he could tolerate.

"I haven't been in touch with him much since he moved to LA. He drunk-dialed me once late at night and I hung up on him."

"Does the symbol of an oval with a horizontal line through the middle of it mean anything to you?"

She paused. "No, I don't think so."

"We think he was going to an exclusive BDSM club called Thanatos here. Did he ever mention that to you? Or do you know if he had friends into the BDSM lifestyle in LA?"

"He had a friend out there who was into that."

Desi felt a jolt. Now she was getting somewhere. This could be a key witness. She poised her pen ready to write.

"Do you have a name?"

"Steve. I don't know his last name. He was Sterling's friend. He did something in movies. That really impressed Sterling. They met at one of these S&M nights when the guy was in New York in business," Shay said.

"What kind of movies? Adult movies?"

"No, it was regular movies, like Hollywood. He managed actors or something like that."

"This could be really important. Could you try and recall a name or number for this guy and get back to me?"

"I'll try."

"Thanks. That's all for now, but I may have to call you back as the investigation progresses."

"Sure."

Desi hung up, deep in thought.

Tenuous connections were floating around the case like loose jellyfish tentacles. She needed the body that connected them all.

"Guess what I found?" Fin broke into her reverie.

"What? That was the ex-fiancée, Shay Stern, by the way."

"Listen to this first. I checked the small print on the back covers of the DVDs. The movies were produced by an outfit called Overexposed Entertainment. I looked up the business filing. The only officer listed is a Harris Feldman. Guess who the registered agent is? Our pal, Martin Groves, the Beverly Hills CPA."

"Maybe he's into the whole S&M scene. Did you get a look at those suspicious-looking marks on his ankles?"

"Wanna bet that Biesu is involved in these movies more than providing a location?" Fin said.

"He's probably financing them. The neighbor described him as a 'pornographer'."

"There's more. I found a website for a Harris Feldman Casting Agency in Chatsworth. It specializes in porn performers."

"Huh. He's got to be linked to Biesu and the performers in the movie. Shay Stern said she broke up with Parker because of his hard-core masochism. He met a guy named Steve from LA, who was into the BDSM scene here and did something in Hollywood with actors. Parker was very impressed with that."

"Steve could be the connect to Thanatos. Maybe even the reason Parker moved out here."

"That's what I'm thinking, but Shay didn't know his last name," Desi said.

"We've got his laptop."

Desi twisted to her desk, booted up Sterling Parker's computer and called up his email. The gmail inbox unscrolled on the screen. She typed "Steve" into the search field for the contact list.

No matches. Then she did the same with his email. The result was the same.

"Nothing," she announced.

"ICE came in," Fin called. "There's no record of a Ruslana Ludmila Cojocaru entering the country. She could be a US national."

"She could be using a fake identity. Anything from those brand manufacturers?"

Fin shook his head. "Two of them said they had nothing. Still waiting on the third. One of the dommes on the DVD covers looks like one of the chicks on the Thanatos website, the one called Achlys. If this Harris Feldman runs a casting agency, he probably put her in the movie and maybe from there she got the gig at Thanatos."

"Makes sense. BDSM is probably a small world. Let's go find Harris Feldman. He's gotta have a line on all this," Desi said. "If we could get Feldman or someone to put Sterling Parker in Biesu's mansion, we've got PC for a warrant."

"Let's do it," Fin said.

The day was typical Southern California—a cloudless sky of cobalt blue.

Desi motored up the 405 freeway to Chatsworth, the epicenter of the nation's adult entertainment industry located in the northern reaches of Los Angeles County.

The dashboard's outside temperature indicator climbed steadily.

It would be at least ten degrees higher in the hinterlands than on LA's Westside, which benefitted from ocean breezes.

"What would you do if you weren't a cop?" Fin asked.

"No idea. I was born to be a rage-filled cop."

"Rage-filled, huh?"

"You don't think you need a sense of rage for this job?"

He nodded.

"Outrage especially. But if you let it, it'll eat you from the inside out until you're a hollow shell."

"That's why I surf." She glanced at him. "What do you do?"

"I paint," he said.

"Paint?"

"Paintings, not houses. I paint oils."

The Blood Room

She glanced at him with fresh interest. "I think you're the first cop artist I've run into. What do you paint, portraits, things like that?"

"I've done portraits, but I like doing landscapes mostly."

"Things that are beautiful inside and out, not like human beings," Desi said.

"You said it. Sometimes I want to totally get away from people, especially my housemates."

"I hear you. For me, it's the ocean," she said. "Art is a nice talent to have. I don't have anything like that."

"Tell the truth, I haven't painted for a while. I kind of lost interest in it."

"Any reason?"

"Not really. Maybe I'll go back to it sometime." He gave a sad smile.

"You should. You can't waste a talent like that."

Desi veered down the exit ramp and turned onto a wide boulevard lined by new housing tracts and shopping centers painted in pastel colors.

"You'd never guess what kind of company town this is," Fin said.

"As long as nobody has to see it, it's tolerated, and it brings jobs," Desi said. "Here it is."

She turned into an office park of modern, low-slung brick buildings bordered with clipped hedges and parked outside the one where the Harris Feldman Agency was located.

The air was pudding thick with the heat of midafternoon and buzzing cicadas. The detectives strode up the sidewalk and into the over air-conditioned building, which made Desi shiver slightly after baking in the sun outside.

The agency was just inside the lobby, identified by its initials on a plate glass window covered with a blind.

She pushed open the door and entered a large reception area of couches where men and women sat, clutching manila envelopes and folders, likely containing headshots, demo reels, and CVs.

They were all wearing snug outfits emphasizing their attributes, décolletages and deltoids, breasts and biceps.

Desi asked to speak with Harris Feldman, flipping open her ID as she did so. The receptionist stared at them with large, round eyes. "Ah, just a moment." He scurried to the back. A few seconds later a short brunette in a pencil skirt tottered out on stiletto heels.

"I'm Christy Vogel. I run the agency. Harris retired a couple years ago."

The detectives looked at each other.

"Then we'd like to ask you some questions in connection with an ongoing investigation, Ms. Vogel," Desi said.

Christy looked at the waiting room. All eyes were fixed on the unfolding scene at the reception counter.

"Come on back," she said.

They settled in a small office, its walls blanketed with framed headshots of porn stars, many scrawled with messages of thanks for career starts.

"What can I help you with?" Christy clasped her hands on her desk.

"Where can we find Harris Feldman?" Desi asked.

"I haven't had any contact with him since I bought the agency, so I don't know if the address and phone number I have for him are still good, but I'll give you what I've got," she said. "He used to live right here in Chatsworth."

She turned to her computer. A moment later, a printer whirred. She reached under her desk and produced a sheet of paper, which she handed to Desi.

"Ms. Vogel, do you know Rory Biesu?" Fin asked.

She blinked just a little too fast. "No, can't say I do."

"Have you heard of him?" Desi said.

"I have. I don't think he's in the business these days."

"So he was?"

"For a short time, I believe."

"Anything else you can tell us about him?"

She shook her head. "Like I said, I don't know him."

"How about a dominatrix named Mistress Achlys?" Desi said.

"I don't handle that genre. I know that was Harris's thing, but I didn't continue it," Christy said.

"How about this guy?" Fin said, pointing to a photo on the wall.

It was a shot of a naked man cupping his genitals with a hand. Flames peeked through and around his fingers. It was the actor from the DVD cover of "The Blood Room."

"Flame?" Christy said. "He's not a current client. That picture was left from Harris's days. I really have to take some of these pictures down."

"You wouldn't know where we could find him?" Fin said.

"Afraid not."

"Why don't you deal with the BDSM genre, Ms. Vogel?" Desi asked.

"I prefer to handle more mainstream projects. The market's bigger and so's the money," she said.

The detectives exchanged a glance. They weren't going to get anything more out of her.

"She's not going to win any Academy Awards for acting," Fin said as they walked back to the car.

"She was lying about Biesu, but I think she was telling the truth about Achlys."

"The question is why?" Fin said. "Let's see if we can confirm this twenty on Harris Feldman."

They got in the car. As Fin called in Feldman's name, Desi cranked the AC. It blasted a stream of stifling air. By the time Fin had finished scribbling on his notepad and hung up, the air had cooled.

"Looks like he's still there. Harris A. Feldman, age sixty-nine."

"Sounds like our man."

"And he's got a prior. Sexual assault and aggravated assault twenty-seven years ago. The charges were dropped."

"This is getting interesting," Desi said. "Rock and roll."

Fin smiled.

"Now you're talking."

Desi's phone bleeped. She checked it. A voicemail had come in during the Vogel interview. She didn't recognize the number, but it was a central LA area code. She pressed play.

As soon as she heard the baritone rumbling voice, the world stopped along with her heartbeat for a millisecond.

"Hey, Desi. I know it's been a while and a lotta shit went down, but I need to talk to you. Can you give me a call?"

Desi immediately hit delete as if some contagious virus had infected her phone. Why the fuck was Rondell Nichols suddenly calling her? He needed to talk to her? Did this have something to do with the bullshit in the newsletter?

"Hey, everything all right?"

She blinked. Fin was staring at her. She was glad she had dark sunglasses on. "Yeah, I'm good."

"You don't look so good."

"I'm fine," she snapped. "Let's go."

She had to get Rondell out of her head. She had let him camp out there long enough in the past. She wasn't going to let him re-establish himself.

They drove out of the office park onto a main boulevard. A large pink neon "XXX" on a side street caught Desi's eye and she swung an abrupt right, halting the car at the curb in front of a hydrant.

Fin looked at her in surprise. "Urgent potty pitstop?"

"Time for some firsthand research," she said, already opening the door.

They strolled into the adult shop, which was full of racy lingerie and adult toys, including, Desi noted, handcuffs and paddles.

A large man with a goatee, his arms sleeved with colorful tattoos, leaned on the counter, engrossed in the centerfold of a skin magazine. Desi pushed her badge over the centerfold into the guy's field of sight as Fin wandered over to a small DVD section.

The guy straightened with a start and flipped the magazine closed.

"Can I help you?" he said, scratching his elbows, which seemed to be a nervous tic judging by the fiery rawness of the skin.

"We're just looking for some general information. Are you the owner here?"

"Yeah, Vinny Spagnolo."

"You ever heard of Overexposed Entertainment?"

"Sure. They did a couple whip-and-chain flicks a few years ago, but they didn't last long. They went out of business."

"You know why?"

He hesitated before talking. "There were rumors that people got hurt on set. They closed it down fast to keep it quiet. They didn't want OSHA coming in."

"You mean hurt in the S&M scenes?"

"Yeah, some of the stuff they did was pretty extreme." He sniffed and rubbed his nose. "I don't know if any of that is true, by the way. It was a couple years ago."

"Extreme, like branding people?"

"I never heard of that specifically, but people are into all kinds of weird shit."

"You sell any of their DVDs?"

He shook his head. "They bought back all their inventory when they shut down. There are newer production companies–filling that niche now and it's all online anyway."

"Is that normal business procedure, to buy back inventory like that?"

"Not really. If companies are going out of business, they're not going to have the cash to buy back their product all over the place, and what are they going to do with all that stuff anyway?" Vinny said.

"You ever heard dommes who go by Mistress Achlys or Odyne?" He shook his head. "How about Flame?"

His face brightened. "Yeah, he was pretty big some years ago, then he 'flamed' out, you might say. I heard he got into ice, bigtime. Now that you mention it, I think he did a couple flicks for

Overexposed. I guess he needed the money, and they probably needed a name star."

"Any idea where we can find him?"

He pursed his lips and scratched his elbows harder. "There's a happy hour every day at a place called No Holds Barred down the street. A lot of the industry crowd hangs out there. You might find him there, or you'll find someone who knows him."

"Thanks, you've been real helpful," Desi said.

The detectives jammed on their sunglasses as they exited the store.

"You get all that?" Desi asked.

"Yeah. Injuries on set and buying back their inventory? Sounds hinky to me," Fin said.

"Sounds more and more like Biesu was behind it. They didn't go out of business because of a lack of cash."

"It could've been because of these injuries. Maybe they had to pay people off," Fin said.

"Let's find Feldman."

Fifteen minutes later, Fin and Desi stood on the wisteria-entwined porch of a wood-frame bungalow. A calico cat was curled up in a swinging chair hanging from the rafters.

"Straight out of a Norman Rockwell painting," Fin said.

Desi rapped the door's brass knocker, which was shaped like a cat's paw.

A spry, sparse-haired man in a plaid cotton shirt and jeans opened. "If you're Jehovah's Witness or Mormons, I'm not interested."

"We're not," Desi said. The detectives held up their badges. "LAPD. Mr. Feldman?"

He gave a terse nod.

"We'd like to ask you about some old clients of yours."

10

Harris Feldman thought for a moment then drew back the door. "Come on in."

Feldman ushered the detectives into a living room where they settled on a chintz-upholstered sofa. He sat in an armchair across from them.

A yawning tabby cat stretched its limbs in a patch of sunlight on the floor next to him. The metronomic ticking of a grandfather clock in a corner of the room was the only sound.

"We just have a few questions in connection with an investigation, Mr. Feldman," Desi said.

"Fire away. Who is it you're looking for?"

"Two dommes, Mistress Achlys and Odyne, who appeared in a couple films produced by your company Overexposed Entertainment."

He scrunched his face in a show of thinking. "Neither of those names ring a bell, but Overexposed hasn't been in production for a few years now."

"Why did it close down?" Desi asked.

"Competition from the Internet. It made money at first, but then it went downhill."

"Did anyone ever get seriously injured on set, Mr. Feldman?" Fin said.

"We had a clean OSHA record. You can look it up."

"Anything that wasn't reported to OSHA?" Desi said.

"Like what, Detective?" Feldman snapped.

"You tell me, Mr. Feldman."

"We ran a clean shop."

Fin jumped in. "Do you know Rory Biesu?"

"He was the principal investor in Overexposed."

"Do you belong to or ever heard of a club called Thanatos?" Fin said.

"This line of questioning has gone a long way off asking about my old clients. What's this really about?" Feldman's demeanor had changed from affable to suspicious to defensive.

"We can't reveal that," Desi said. "It's an ongoing investigation."

"In that case, I think I've answered your questions." He stood, indicating the interview was at an end, and ushered them out to the hallway.

The wall in front of them was jammed ceiling to floor with framed photos of varying sizes. It was behind the front door, so it hadn't been visible when they entered. The detectives stopped to scan them. A younger Feldman starred in almost all the pictures, striking poses with chesty, chiseled beauties.

Standing off to the side, Fin tilted his head at Desi as he threw a sideways glance at Feldman, a signal that he wanted her to distract Feldman's attention. What was he doing?

"Was Flame one of your clients?" Desi said. Feldman turned to face her as Fin turned back to face the wall.

"He was for a time."

"Any idea where we can find him?"

"I haven't had anything to do with him for a long time. I haven't the foggiest."

"One last question, Mr. Feldman?" Impatience crossed his face. Desi ignored it. "Why did Overexposed buy back all the DVDs when it went out of business?"

"That's proprietary and confidential information."

Fin gave a brief nod. All clear.

The detectives said nothing until they shut themselves inside the car. Fin immediately took out his cell phone.

"There was a framed newspaper-type photo of Feldman with one of the dommes on the wall. I think it's a young version of Achlys. I took a picture of it." He enlarged the screen with his fingers and read.

Agent Harris Feldman at the annual adult entertainment industry banquet with one of his stars, Sweetbriar.

He handed her the phone. Desi studied the grainy black and white photo. "It does look a little like her. She might have changed her stage name, especially if she wasn't doing the BDSM stuff before." She handed the phone back to Fin and took out her cell phone to check messages.

"You want to hit that happy hour?" Fin said. "We're right on time."

Desi was listening to a voicemail. She clicked off and lowered the phone. "Shay Stern. She got Parker's friend's last name. It's Wu, W-U, Steve Wu."

Fin was already typing into his phone. He waited a beat. "Got him. Steve Wu, an agent with Artistic Representations in Century City," he said. "He represents some pretty big names in Hollywood."

"That must be him. Shay said he managed actors. No wonder Thanatos is a secret club."

Fin checked his watch. "Shit. We should get there before the agency closes for the day," he said.

"What about the happy hour? If we miss it today, we'll have to wait another day."

Fin thought for a moment. "How 'bout I do Wu and you stick around and see what you get from the happy hour? I'll come back and get you."

"Done," Desi said.

"That way, I'll at least get to eat."

Desi gave a wry smile. "You could stand to lose a few pounds."

"You don't hold back, Detective Nimmo."
"Then we make a good team, Detective McNab."

Customers were trickling into No Holds Barred, but they weren't stopping in the dining area. They were passing through to the rear of the restaurant. Desi finished her BLT sandwich and sat back, looking down a hallway. There had to be another room where the porn happy hour was being held.

After paying the bill, she joined the parade. The rear door opened on to a patio surrounded by a high bamboo fence and furnished with umbrella-topped tables and potted palms. Strings of fairy lights hung over the area, which buzzed with low chatter from the tables.

"I'm sorry. This area's reserved." A waiter stood at Desi's elbow. "I can get you a table inside."

She flipped open his ID. "Police business," she said. The waiter backed off quietly.

Desi approached the first table and introduced herself. "I'm trying to locate a couple performers known as Sweetbriar or Mistress Achlys and a guy named Flame, old clients of Harris Feldman. They're not in any trouble. I just need to ask them a couple questions for background in an investigation."

"Sweetbriar? Wasn't she involved in that HIV scare a few years back?" An older man asked the table.

"Yeah, that was her. She got blacklisted and fell on hard times. That was the last I heard of her," a woman with long platinum curls said.

"Any idea what her real name is?" Desi asked.

They shook their heads.

"I know someone who worked with her on a movie. Hold on." A man with a bad toupée took out a phone and keyed in a text. He looked up as he tossed the phone on the table. "Why don't you sit down and have a drink?"

"Thanks, but I'm on duty," Desi said.

"Come back when you're off," he retorted with a sly smile.

She tweaked her lips in response and moved to another table to repeat her spiel.

A skinny guy, maybe early twenties with a couple pimples on his chin, darted his eyes away from her at the mention of Flame. Desi kept him in her peripheral vision as she spoke to the others.

"Flame ain't been around here for a while," a stocky man said. "I don't even know if he's still in the business."

"Shame. He had a good gimmick going with those tatts," a woman said with a laugh.

"The flames are tattoos?" Desi said. "I wondered about that."

"Sure are."

"Better him than me," a bald man said.

"Anyone ever work on an Overexposed Entertainment movie?" Desi said.

The question landed like a lump of concrete. People averted their eyes, sipped their drinks.

She pressed. "I heard there were a lot of safety issues on the set."

No one answered. The jovial tone had frozen over.

Desi distributed her business cards around the table. No one picked them up. "Just in case you think of something, give me a bell."

The kid was working hard at scraping the label off his beer bottle with a forefinger nail. He knew something.

She returned to the first table. "Anything from your friend?" she asked the hairpiece.

"Nope but give me your card. I'll let you know."

"You investigating Harris Feldman by any chance?" the bearded guy asked as she handed out her cards.

Desi looked at him with interest. "I can't say, but why do you ask?"

"A cop was looking into him one time, a few years ago, but nothing happened." He frowned. "If I remember right, it had something to do with employing illegal immigrants."

"Got a name on the cop?" Desi said. "Were they from ICE?"

He shook his head. "It was one of your guys, though, LAPD."

"Too bad they didn't get him," another man muttered.

Desi twisted toward him.

"What do you mean?"

"Rex," the woman with the curls said in a cautionary tone.

"Just that," Rex said.

They had closed ranks again. What was the deal with Feldman?

Desi walked out of the restaurant, ducking into the doorway of an adjacent bookstore to check her cell phone.

Feldman had caught police attention before. For illegal immigration? That was a federal matter, falling under the jurisdiction of Immigration and Customs Enforcement. LAPD didn't investigate illegal immigrants. The guy could have mixed up his agencies, but he seemed positive it was LAPD.

Chatsworth fell under the purview of LAPD's Devonshire Division, otherwise known as "Club Dev." It was a small area with less crime than West LA. That would've been the most likely source of the cop unless it was one of the specialized downtown units.

Even if it was downtown or a federal investigation, someone in Club Dev should have a line on the investigation. Did she know anyone over there in detectives? A personal connection always helped.

As she was wracking her memory, the jumpy kid emerged from No Holds Barred.

Desi straightened. The kid jogged across the street and got into a battered Honda.

She took off to corral him, but she was hampered by a rush of oncoming traffic. By the time she reached the other side, the kid was zooming out of the parking space.

She squinted and caught his license plate. She called it in for a run on the number. In a minute, the information came back.

The car was registered to Jason Niedermeier with an address in San Fernando, a low-rent town nearby. Then Desi called Club Dev and asked if a patrol car was available to give a car-less detective an assist.

The Blood Room

Jason Niedermeier's address led Desi to a block of shabby duplexes where grass struggled to grow on the dusty ground amid a tangle of desiccated vine inside chain link fences.

She told the patrol officer who had given her a lift to wait at the car. She didn't want the uniform to alarm Niedermeier. She'd call the officer if she needed backup.

A volley of voices in rat-a-tat Spanish and a baby's cry floated out of neighboring windows as she approached the door. She rapped it hard.

Niedermeier opened the door, releasing an odorous cloud of stale beer and pot. Shock registered on his face when he saw her.

"Mr. Niedermeier, I believe we just met."

"What do you want?"

"Where's Flame?"

"Like I told you, I don't ..."

"I know you know where he is. If you lie to me, I will book you."

"I ain't got nothing to hide from the five-o," came a robust voice from the apartment's interior. A biracial man, half Asian, half black, with bleached white hair, high cheekbones and dark pits for eyes appeared next to Niedermeier.

He was shirtless, wearing baggy green nylon basketball shorts and metal rings through his nipples. The tips of his famed tattooed flames peeked above his low-slung waistband. "What's this about?"

"You're Flame?" He answered yes with a jerk of his chin. "I just want to ask you about a couple movies you did a few years ago."

"You better come in. I don't need people seeing the po-po on my porch," Flame said, opening the door wider and shunting Niedermeier aside. "It's all right," he murmured. Niedermeier brushed Flame's waist with a protective palm. They were lovers.

As Desi stepped into the apartment, Flame craned his neck outside to see if anyone was observing before shutting the door.

Bottles clinked. Niedermeier was cleaning up the remnants of a party in the living room. It was a bigger job than he had time for.

The coffee table was scattered with ash, a packet of rolling papers was strewn on the floor. Beer bottles huddled on a counter separating the kitchen and living area.

"So which movie we talkin' about?" Flame sat in an armchair and fired up a cigarette, tossing the lighter onto the coffee table with a clatter. Desi perched herself on the edge of a stained sofa.

" 'The Blood Room'."

Flame scratched his chin. "Oh yeah. That one."

Desi asked him his legal name. "Owen Kidd. But I go by Flame, period."

" 'The Blood Room' was filmed at a mansion in Holmby Hills, right?"

"Yeah, some rich dude who's into all that BDSM shit. He had his own personal dungeon in the basement."

"Did you see any branding going on there?"

"Branding?"

"Burning someone with a hot iron."

Flame winced. "That's extreme, man. No, I never seen nothing like that. There was a scene in one of the movies I did where I had to fake burning someone with a hot poker, but we didn't actually do it. You could just hear the guy screaming like he was being burned."

"Did you ever see anything like a branding iron there? A long metal rod with some kind of symbol on the end?"

"Can't recall no branding iron. It was a while ago. I do recall he had a whole lotta that shit, some nasty lookin' stuff. Just so's you know, I ain't personally into that scene. I needed the cash, so I did the work." He jabbed his cigarette in the air as he spoke. Bits of ash flew off.

"Can you think back a little harder?" Desi pressed. "Was there any talk about branding people or maybe a propane torch?"

Flame's face cleared. "We used a welder's torch for the poker scene."

Desi noted that. "You ever run into a Mistress Achlys or a Mistress Odyne?"

"Achlys is a domme. She works at the mansion."

"You mean the mansion where you shot the movie?"

"What other one I been talking about?"

"What do you mean by 'works'?"

"The guy who owns the mansion runs these S&M parties there. I work them every now and then when I need the cash. My agent gets me the jobs."

"Harris Feldman?"

"Yeah."

He leaned forward and tapped his ash in an overflowing ashtray.

"Rory Biesu, that name mean anything to you?" Desi said.

Flame shook his head as Desi took out her phone and showed Sterling Parker's face to him. "Recognize him at all?"

"Nope." He was either a good liar or telling the truth.

"Who's at these parties?"

"The clients wear masks. I got the impression it's a lot of rich people who don't want to be recognized."

"Where can I find Achlys?"

"Couldn't tell you. Your best bet is at the next party at that place."

"How about her real name?"

He shook his head. "No one gives their real names in that biz."

"Why did Feldman shut down Overexposed Entertainment and get out of movies?"

Flame shrugged. "Guess he got tired of it. He sold his agency, too."

"You ever hear anything about safety issues on set?"

He shook his head. "Harris ran a tight operation. He was above board on everything. Where'd you hear there were safety issues?"

"Around. How about employing illegal immigrants?"

Flame blew out a stream of smoke. "He'd be blackballed if he did that. No one would work for him. Detective, there's a lot of jealousy in this business. You can't always believe what you hear."

11

Ⓗ

Fin was quite happy to have split from Desi for the moment. He needed to get his head together, figure out how he could leap ahead in the investigation. Desi seemed to have lowered her guard with him.

That was a good first step, but he needed more, he needed to make the case his. Truth be told, though, he was feeling just a tiny pinprick of guilt. He had come to grudgingly like his new partner. She was a good detective. But he couldn't let emotion stand in his way. He had a mission to accomplish.

He made good time heading south into the city until he got off the freeway on Santa Monica Boulevard, when he slammed into the muddy morass of city traffic.

He flicked on the flashing grill lights and managed to shove the Crown Vic through the tide of vehicles to the huddle of tall office buildings known as Century City.

He pulled up in front of a white, modernistic building with an abstract sculpture in a front courtyard.

The scripted monogram "AR" crowned a doorway where a cluster of parking valets, clad in dazzling white Bermuda shorts and sneakers, hovered like a swarm of bees.

One of them dashed up as Fin parked the car in the crescent-moon driveway. He flashed his ID at him.

"Police business," he said in an authoritative tone. "You can leave it here."

The valet skidded to a halt and nodded.

Fin entered the building and crossed a grey-veined marble lobby dotted with white orchids to a long desk with a row of receptionists like bank tellers and asked for Mr. Wu. The receptionist's face dropped when Fin announced who he was.

Fin had to admit he always enjoyed the badge effect. For those with nothing to hide, the reaction was deference. For those with something to hide, it was often defiance. Both were driven by fear.

The badge was power.

As the guy burbled into the phone, Fin milled around the lobby. Elegantly dressed people marched with purpose in and out. A man with an actor's tan and square jaw entered. Fin recognized him as one of the stars from "The Narc Files" TV show. His housemates would get a kick out of that.

A young man with skinny leg jeans and his hair coiffed into a gelled meringue on top of his head emerged from an elevator and headed purposefully toward him. "Detective McNab? I'll take you up to Mr. Wu."

Five minutes later, Steve Wu, dressed in a natty bright blue suit with an open collar, combed back an errant curl of hair that dropped over his forehead as his assistant closed his office door behind Fin.

"Detective, I take it you're here about Milo Milovich. What's my bad boy client done now?" he said in a jocular tone as he sat behind a desk, leaning back in a chrome and leather chair and crossing his legs.

"I'm here about Sterling Parker." Fin trained his eyes on him. He was rewarded when the bonhomie slid right off the agent's face and into his lap.

"Sterling?"

"He's a friend of yours, right?"

"Yes, but what …?"

"I'm sorry to have to inform you, but he was found dead earlier this week."

"Oh my god, I didn't know."

"We're investigating his death. It's routine procedure in cases like these," Fin said.

"This is a shock. What happened?"

"I can't go into details, but he was found dead in an alley in West LA. How long have you known Sterling?"

Wu looked dazed then shook his head as if to come out of it. "Sorry. I'm just ... Not that long. We met in New York. Then he moved out here."

"How did you meet him originally?"

He cast his eyes at his desk and rubbed the cleft in his chin. "Ah, how did we meet?" he muttered. He looked up with the answer rolling off his tongue. "At a club."

"What kind of club?"

He half smiled. "I'm a little embarrassed to say."

"I'm not here to judge, Mr. Wu. I just need you to tell the truth."

"It was a sex club."

"A BDSM sex club?"

He hesitated. "You could say that," he said.

"When Sterling came out here, he looked you up, as would be natural since he didn't know many people here." Wu nodded. "Did you guys talk about a similar kind of club here that Sterling could join?"

"I'm kind of out of that stuff right now."

"But did you talk about it?"

"I don't really remember. We may have, but what does this have to do with anything?"

"Are you a member of 'Thanatos'?" Fin said, slicing through the non-answers.

Wu paled.

Fin had found the connect.

Steve Wu's eyes widened slightly. "Isn't Thanatos something in Greek mythology?"

He was playing for time. The name meant something more to him than mythology. "You've never heard of a club called Thanatos?"

"Not that I can recall." Light from the window highlighted the sheen that had spread in a film across his forehead.

It was time to rattle him a little. "Mr. Wu, misrepresentation to a police officer is a crime."

"Actually, now that I think of it, I have heard of a club called that, yes."

"Are you a member?"

He gathered himself. "I haven't done anything illegal, Detective, but before we go any further, I'd like to consult my attorney."

Damn it. The interview was over. Fin handed him a business card.

"If you could have your attorney contact me at his or her earliest convenience, then we can finish this conversation and you can be rid of me."

He gave Wu a saccharin smile, and Wu bid his assistant to escort Fin to the front door of the building.

With a nod at the parking valet, Fin got in the Crown Vic. Steve Wu was the Thanatos link.

It was too bad he lawyered up. But he was soft. Hauling him down to the station might shake him up enough to crack, even with a lawyer.

Fin started the car. He suddenly couldn't face driving all the way back to Chatsworth then back down to West LA then home to Riverside. He texted Desi.

Can you get a ride back? Wu lied when he denied Thanatos then lawyered up. I'm beat.

The reply came within a couple seconds. Go on home. See you tomorrow.

That was a relief. He headed to the station.

Desi jammed the phone into her jacket pocket and looked at Detective José María Mondragón, who was sipping a sugar-free Red Bull.

They were in the squad room at the Devonshire Division station where she had the patrol car drop her after the interview with Flame.

It was smaller than West LA's, and a lot newer. It looked more like an insurance office than a cop shop.

"What was that name again?" Mondragón said, trying to squelch a belch at the same time.

"Harris Feldman. Porn agent and producer. Lives in Chatsworth. I was told that one of our guys was poking around about him a couple years ago, something about illegal immigrants. I figured that was likely someone from here."

Mondragón turned to his computer. He had a sign on his desk that said "Hecho en México." Made in Mexico, likely to counteract the impression that he was white due to his freckle-sprayed alabaster skin and reddish-chestnut hair.

"How do you figure this guy Feldman in your case?" Mondragón said.

"Not sure. All I know is that his name keeps coming up. Thought it was worth checking out."

"I bet it was Al Hargitay. Sounds like one of his cases. He handles a lot of the stuff connected to the porn industry. He's out on disability."

Figured. Desi rubbed her forehead then looked up. "Got a home number for him?"

"I'll do better than that. I'm off in five minutes. I'll take you to him."

Dusk was stealing the day by the time Desi and Mondragón strode up the driveway of a two-story house in a cookie-cutter development. Al Hargitay lived out in the scrubby rolling hills of Ventura County's Simi Valley, a sun-battered area that bordered LA County on the north.

It was pocked with modern shopping centers with red-tile roofs and housing developments landscaped with drought-resistant cactus and agave plants along roads designed to be attractively winding. The city had proven to be a popular residential area for LAPD cops, far enough away from the craziness of urban streets but within a semi-reasonable commuting distance. The suburban sterility was not for Desi.

Al Hargitay answered the door in a back brace.

"Hey, Al," Mondragón said.

"Dragon. Thought I'd never say I was glad to see your ugly mug."

"Same here, girlfriend. Squad's not the same without you."

Hargitay invited them in. Desi introduced herself as she stepped out of the well-baked air into the cooled comfort of air conditioning with relief. "Thanks for seeing me on such short notice."

"You're doing me the favor, believe me. I'm climbing the walls stuck at home."

Hargitay shuffled into a family room dominated by a seventy-two-inch TV displaying the chattering heads of a sports talk show and plonked into an armchair that appeared to be his nest. A wall of shelves bore colorful ceramic pots, vases, and figurines. He grabbed the remote and muted the TV.

He was stocky, mid-fifties with a florid face and spider's web of broken capillaries on his nose, caused by booze Desi judged by the two beer cans sitting on a small table next to the chair.

"Take a seat. You want something to drink?"

"I'll take water," Desi said.

"I can do better than that. Deb, bring some lemonade!"

"Brewsky for me. I'm officially off-duty," Mondragón said.

"How'd you hurt your back?" Desi asked.

"Stupid shit. Clearing junk out of the garage. Picked up a box and there it went. Agony." They small-talked a little more before curiosity drove Hargitay to the point. "What's the urgent case you're working?"

Desi filled him in on the details as Hargitay gulped the last of his beer.

A woman with too-blond hair and a lined face appeared with a tray bearing a glass of lemonade and two tall beer cans.

The glass was streaked with dun-colored mud. Deb Hargitay wiped it off with a mud-spattered apron before she handed it to Desi. Her hands and fingernails were encrusted with dirt.

"Sorry. It's clay. I'm a potter. It's dirty work."

'You made all these pots?" Desi said as she accepted the drink.

Deb beamed. "Yes. I sell them at craft shows."

Desi nodded appreciatively. "They're very nice."

"I'll leave you to it," Deb said.

Hargitay and Mondragón grabbed cans and popped the tops with successive, loud cracks.

"Who's your source for all this?" Hargitay said.

"People in the porn industry."

Hargitay signaled for her to divulge more details.

She paused.

"Guy in an adult toy store, but some others …"

Hargitay waved his hand in the air. "Rumors. I've been around this business a long time and wasted a lot of time checking out hearsay and rumors. There's a lot of jealousy and people will say anything."

That had become a familiar refrain.

Hargitay chuckled dryly. "I checked out Feldman a couple years ago and didn't find anything. Don't waste your time."

"I guess I already have," she said.

"You came to the right person then," Hargitay said. "I'll save you from wasting more."

"Why is everyone afraid of Feldman?"

Hargitay shrugged grandly. "No idea. He's a harmless old perv."

"You ever come across a porn producer called Rory Biesu, Romanian national?"

Hargitay made a show of considering the name. "Biesu … nope."

Desi studied Hargitay.

Something about his blanket dismissiveness irked her. She didn't want to ask him anything else. Her gut told her he would wave off all other questions.

"Well, I guess that's it." Desi looked at Mondragón.

They chitchatted a few more minutes, complaining about the latest departmental policies, bandying names about to see if they knew any people in common until Desi deemed enough time had passed to seem polite.

"I have a long ride home, so I better get going. Thanks for the help," she said.

They stood and walked to the front door. Night had dropped its curtain, but light beamed onto the driveway from the open garage door, which displayed a large, gleaming boat. Next to it was a Tesla. Neither sold for less than a hundred grand.

"Nice toys," Desi said. "I bet those cost you plenty of OT."

"I made a couple good investments. That's the only way to make real money," Hargitay said.

"It's the squad party boat," Mondragón said. "We've had some good times on her."

"Where do you go with it?" Desi said.

"Up and down the coast, out to Catalina."

"Put me on your guest list sometime."

"As soon as I get this brace off."

They said goodbye. Desi turned to descend the driveway. As she opened the door to Mondragón's car, she looked back at the house. The garage door was closing.

Desi trudged up the stairs to the West LA squad room. It was quiet.

Keisha looked up from her computer. "You look beat."

"Does it show that much?"

"Yep. You hungry? Stamos left me some moussaka. His mom made it."

"Greek comfort food?"

"I was just about to take a dinner break. Come on. I'll give you some." Keisha stood and led the way into the kitchen, where she opened the fridge, took out a plastic container and slid it into the microwave.

"I'm not hungry, but I'll sit with you," Desi said. She poured herself a coffee and sat at the table.

Greek. The whole Greek mythology thing connected to Thanatos was weird. What was up with that? There was something else though, that lurked in the fuzzy recesses of her mind, the edges of which she couldn't grasp. She was too tired to think so she gave up.

"What are you doing so late here tonight anyway?" Desi said.

"Filling in for Len. He had to take a personal day. Some problem with his daughter."

"Relapse?"

"Sounded like it."

Desi shook her head. "Poor Len. He's spent a fortune on rehabs for that kid."

Keisha took the moussaka out from the microwave and pulled up a chair. "How's McNab?"

"He's actually working out pretty well. It's cool having a partner again. Forgot what it was like."

"Don't get too warm and fuzzy. I get the feeling you need to watch your back with him."

"What do you mean?"

"He was in here cozying up to the LT this morning. I saw him watch her come in and then he made a beeline in right after her."

Desi sipped her coffee. "The LT seems to have a thing for him."

"All she cares about is getting clearance rates up and crime numbers down. Remember that." Keisha got up and fetched a fork from the dish drying rack. "Try it." She handed the fork to Desi and pushed her plate closer.

Desi sawed off a wedge and tasted the eggplant and meat casserole. "Hey, this is good."

"Stamos will be thrilled. You should head over to The Shop, unwind a little."

It sounded like a good idea. "You know I think I'll do that. I haven't had a beer for a while."

"Have one for me, girl."

The nondescript local cop watering hole lay just around the corner from the station on Santa Monica Boulevard. Its nameless ruddy brick exterior was interrupted by a metal door flanked by two small windows like eyes.

Over the past couple months, taggers had discovered its status as a cop hangout, which had made it a premium graffiti target. As she walked up, Desi noticed they'd been at it again. A jumble of black chicken-scratch tags fringed the wall along the sidewalk, a banner of defiance and rebellion.

She pulled open the door and stepped into an amniotic-warm atmosphere of dim light and a soft Bob Seger tune playing on an old jukebox. Balls clicked on the pool table at the back.

A quick survey confirmed that the ten or so patrons were all cops.

Harry Blaze, the bartender with a bowling ball belly, was polishing the old wooden bar, running a towel over it in huge circular sweeps, as he always did between orders. She slid onto a stool.

He looked up, his beetled eyebrows raised in a question, and she raised a finger at him. A moment later, a cold-misted beer came gliding down the bar. She caught it in a cupped palm.

"Rough day?" Harry said, ambling down the aisle behind the bar to catch up with the bottle.

"Just long." She took a deep draft. "Looks like the taggers got you again."

"Tell me about it. I'm going to have to plant ivy to cover the walls, but it'll ruin my gritty rep, make this look like a decent place."

She smiled and sipped her beer. "Don't worry, Harry. Your secret's safe with a bunch of cops."

He shambled off to serve a customer at the other end of the bar.

She took a long swallow of beer. She could feel the Sterling Parker investigation stalling.

Every lead was turning into a dead end. Every witness was lawyering up or not talking. She needed something to come through.

Just one small break. If it didn't happen soon, Butler would make her put the case on ice and work one of the old cases she'd handed to McNab.

Her phone buzzed with an incoming text.

Call me. Please. It's all good. R.

Fuck him. She tossed her phone on the bar as if it singed her fingers.

It buzzed again. She ignored it and foraged in her purse for change for the jukebox.

"You're not going to get that?" a familiar voice asked.

A hand slid the phone in front of her. She forgot the voice as she saw the text was from the 818 area code. The San Fernando Valley. Not Rondell Nichols. She picked up the phone and read it.

Her name is Bryony Podeswa, and according to my friend, a nasty piece of work who deserves whatever she has coming. BTW, you didn't hear it from me.

It had to be from the guy from the porn happy hour. He'd tracked down Mistress Achlys.

"Good news?"

Desi looked up to see a face from her past smiling at her.

"Holy shit, Denny Comiskey!"

"Long time no see, huh?"

"A lifetime." Desi felt the spark of the crush she'd had on him way back at the academy.

"I'm over in Pacific now, heading up a new detail on biker gangs. Los Federales just moved into Venice."

"That's my hood."

"You live in Venice?"

She nodded. "You're working with the ATF on that?"

"As little as possible. You know the feds. We do the grunt work then they bigfoot the case and get all the glory."

Desi nodded dumbly, feeling the rush of an embarrassing memory. The last time she'd seen Denny was a drunken night in a bar when she'd begged him to keep seeing her after he'd jilted her to go back to an old girlfriend.

She'd grabbed his arm, which he lifted out of her clutch as if she were a leper. A friend of his standing nearby counseled her to let him go. She did.

"You still married to ... Lisa, was that her name?"

"Good memory." Denny ran his fingers through a coxcomb of grey-flecked hair. "Divorced. Then remarried. Then redivorced."

A typical cop story. "Kids?"

"Two from the first, one from the second. You?"

"Still single after all these years," she said.

"That's good," he said in a low tone. He lifted his voice. "Hey, take you on in darts?"

She grabbed her beer and slid off the stool. "You realize you're on my turf, homeboy."

"I know it. Hey, Harry, another pitcher," Denny called.

"I see you're already best buds with Harry."

"Always make nice to the bartender, that's my motto."

He introduced her to his buddies, three dicks and a sergeant from Pacific.

"How come you guys are slumming it in West Latte?" she asked. They exchanged coy smiles.

"We're checking out departmental watering holes one by one," offered a stringbean of a guy named Bruce Savage.

"You mean the badge bunny action," Desi said.

"Something like that," the sarge said.

Denny laughed. "You're the same, Desi. You never miss a trick."

"Oh, I miss plenty."

"Hey, Den, you're up," Savage said.

Denny put down his glass, gathered a handful of darts, tossed. He got within a centimeter of the bullseye, which provoked a chorus of "ooh's."

He plucked out the darts and handed them to Desi.

She aimed carefully and threw a surprisingly straight shot given the pleasant fuzziness in her brain. It thudded just outside the red dot's border.

"You always had a good aim," Denny said.

"Hey, did I tell you guys about the death-by-Viagra stiff today?" The sergeant wiped the foam sliding down the side of his beer glass with a forefinger.

"This transient croaked on Venice Beach. He had a major flagpole in his pants."

"A stiff with a stiff?" Savage said.

"At least he died happy," Denny said.

"Maybe that's what happens to those towel-heads when they blow themselves up dreaming of forty virgins in paradise," another guy said.

"Speaking of virgins in paradise ..." Savage's gaze was directed to the door where three bottle-blondes had just walked in. "Hey, girls, play darts?" he called too loudly.

"No virgins there, guaranteed," Desi said.

Denny lowered his voice. "Hey, you wanna get out of here?" She felt herself melting but halted herself. She wasn't going there with him or anybody else ever again in the department.

"I'm working a big case," she said. "I gotta be in early tomorrow."

"Is that an excuse?"

"What if it is?"

"Then I'm not giving up."

She set down her beer bottle. "Good seeing you, Denny."

"You'll be seeing more of me soon," he called as she walked out. She waved without turning around.

She walked back to her car amid wisps of mist, feeling a burn of warmth inside her.

It felt good to be wanted. But dating cops, even one-night flings, was a mistake she couldn't allow herself to make ever again.

Denny, in fact, had been her first lesson. Too bad she hadn't learned from it by the time she got to Hollywood. She had followed her heart too many times. Now she had to think before acting. She drove home and sank into bed.

Desi awoke with a start, an image of Sterling Parker's brand mark stamping the darkness in front of her eyes. She must've been dreaming about the case. Then she felt that magic click of neural connection. Greek mythology. Of course.

Desi flung off the covers and padded to the kitchen, where her laptop sat on the table. She powered it on and typed in several search terms. A list of symbols popped up. She scanned them. There it was.

The zero with the horizontal line. It was a Greek letter, theta. Corresponds to the English 'th,' as in 'thick' or 'thin'. Or Thanatos.

She sat back. That was it. That was the connection between the Sterling Parker's brand and Thanatos and Rory Biesu.

She now had probable cause for a search warrant of Biesu's mansion.

12

When Fin arrived at six the next morning, he was surprised—and slightly disconcerted—to see Desi poring over her computer amid the sound of clacking keys. He noted her damp, frizzing hair and the dark patch on the shoulders of her blouse. She'd rushed out of the house.

"You're in early. What's up?" he said.

Desi paused her typing and leaned back in her chair.

"I'm writing up the search warrant for Biesu. I found the connection between Thanatos and Sterling Parker's fatal injury."

He hiked his eyebrows.

"Which is?"

"The brand symbol is the Greek letter for 'th,' as in 'thanatos.'"

Fin nodded. Dammit. Why hadn't he thought of that?

"Makes sense. Good going."

"I owe John Stamos and his mom's moussaka for that one. It got me thinking Greek, but unfortunately not until the wee hours. And I have Mistress Achlys's name: Bryony Podeswa. A contact at the porn happy hour came through last night."

"You're on a roll."

He tried to inject brightness into his voice but was aware how flat he sounded.

"I gotta get coffee," he said, hoping that would account for his lack of enthusiasm.

"I'm hoping this is the break we need." Desi hunched over the keyboard again. "Check out Podeswa, see if we can get an address on her. I want to file this warrant ASAP, and then we'll go pay a visit to our favorite dominatrix."

"To save time, I could go bring her in while you finish the warrant," Fin said. "It might be good to grab her now."

Desi's gaze felt like barbed wire on him. Was she back to being prickly again? "I'm nearly done. Somehow I don't get the feeling she's an early riser." Yep, she was back to being prickly again. He had lost ground overnight.

"Sure." Fin wandered off to the break room, poured himself coffee and leafed through the morning's copy of the newspaper lying on the table, then returned at his desk. Desi had written the name "Bryony Podeswa" on a piece on paper and left it on his keyboard.

He plugged the name into the database. According to DMV records, Bryony Podeswa, age forty-six, lived in the seedy neighborhood of East Hollywood, on the other side of the city.

Her priors filled the screen: drunk and disorderly, two narcotics possessions and possession with intent, petty theft, burglary second degree, battery, misrepresentation to a peace officer.

She did time on the narc charges twelve years ago. It was a regular addict jacket. Hardly a surprise.

He sat staring at the screen. If he was going to bounce out of West LA, he needed the case to be higher profile. He had to figure out something and fast.

As the detectives cut across town on Santa Monica Boulevard, the neighborhoods grew downscale, and storefronts filled with signs and billboards in Spanish and Thai.

Fin groaned as he halted the plain wrap at yet another red light. "Podeswa would have to live all the way over here."

"Cheap rent," Desi said.

"I guess Biesu's the only one who rakes in the dough in the beat-me-whip-me business," Fin said.

"From her list of priors, she's lucky to be employed at all," Desi said. "I can't wait to show up and shove the warrant in his face."

"That was solid deduction about the Greek letter. Sherlock would be proud," Fin said.

"Don't patronize me, McNab. I know how to do my job," Desi snapped.

She really was in a bearish mood this morning.

Desi's phone dinged. She studied her phone and looked up. "The DA signed off on the warrant. She's taking it up to the judge. By the time we get through with Podeswa, we should know if we got it or not."

Fin didn't answer. He wasn't going to risk saying the wrong thing again. A curtain of awkward silence dropped between them. Fin grew pensive.

The press still hadn't got wind of a body found in West LA. He listened to the all-news radio station every morning and evening on his commute, and there'd been no mention of it. He hadn't seen it in the newspaper.

Media relations must not have issued a release on it. If they had, the press would've picked it up. The discovery of a body on the Westside was news.

An idea occurred to him, one that would immediately generate buzz about the case.

What was the name of that reporter who covered police and crime news? The one who had written what had seemed to him like an avalanche of articles about his own case.

Fin had no great affection for reporters, but if the media had used him for headlines, he could use them.

Desi pointed at a sign coming up. "Here's Podeswa's street."

Fin turned off the boulevard into a street lined with shabby bungalows, pickup trucks, and trees whose roots had turned the sidewalk into an undulating ribbon. Bryony Podeswa's address led them to a concrete driveway tufted with weeds and grass pushing through cracks.

A dark blue Corolla, pockmarked with rough pink patches of amateur body repair, was parked in the driveway that ended in a garage that had been converted into a small dwelling.

Fin pulled into the driveway, and they got out, pushing open a chain-link gate bearing a mailbox and a chipped-paint sign: *Cuidado: Perro Bravo.* Beware: Angry Dog. The cloying scent of fried food hung in the air. A Mexican ranchera wailed from an unseen radio.

"You want to do the talking?" Fin said.

"Be my guest."

The entrance was on the side of the garage. Desi positioned herself so she'd be able to get a look through the door when it opened.

Fin rapped on the metal border of the screen door. "Ms. Podeswa, police. Open up." He waited a moment, then rapped again, harder, and raised his tone. "Police!"

"All right already. I'm coming," came a tobacco-hoarsened voice edged with irritation. The interior door swung open. A woman wedged herself in the gap. Her eyes bounced between the two detectives. Desi couldn't see anything past her but a dim interior.

"Yeah?" Bryony Podeswa's face was pasty white, full of hard angles and crevices from drug use that made her look a decade older than her age. Her hair was wrapped in a towel turban. The rest of her was clothed in short shorts and a tank top.

The tip of an angry-red scar peeked above the scoop neckline and her breasts swung loose under it.

The detectives introduced themselves, badged her and gave their usual spiel of needing information in connection with a routine investigation. She scowled.

"You think I'm gonna fall for that shit? You ain't got nothing on me 'cos I ain't done nothing."

"You work as a dominatrix for Rory Biesu and Thanatos?" Fin said.

Bryony's eyes were black coins. "I ain't talking to you without a lawyer, so fuck off." She slammed the door. Fin wedged his business card into the jamb.

"We'll have to do this at the station then, Bryony. Have your lawyer give us a call," he called. "We'll be back with a patrol car if we don't hear from you by tomorrow."

The detectives walked back to the car. Fin jutted a thumb at the dog sign. "The only angry dog in there is Bryony Podeswa. You see anything at all?"

"Nope, but I bet we found our brander," Desi said getting in the passenger seat. "If anyone could stick a hot metal rod onto someone's flesh, it would be her."

Fin turned the ignition and backed out into the street. "I'm with you on that one. She's hard as they come. Shit, we came all this way for nothing."

Desi checked her email as they pulled onto Santa Monica Boulevard. "Hey, the judge signed the warrant. We're on."

"Hallelujah. Let's get this asshole Biesu ASAP."

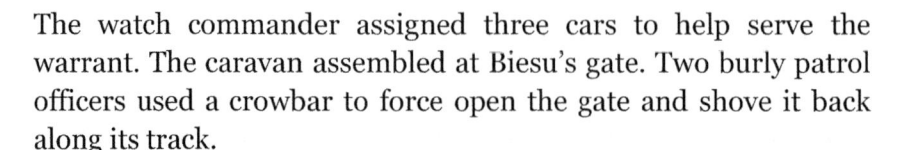

The watch commander assigned three cars to help serve the warrant. The caravan assembled at Biesu's gate. Two burly patrol officers used a crowbar to force open the gate and shove it back along its track.

Desi zoomed through in the plain wrap, followed by the patrol cars, and came to an abrupt halt in front of the steps. She barreled out through the door and bounded up the steps to the front door.

The patrol officers trotted behind her, carrying a small battering ram to break the door lock if no one answered.

She hammered the door with her fist. "LAPD! Open up!"

She waited only a few seconds then stood aside for the uniforms to charge forward with the battering ram. The door splintered under the first blow. Officers blasted in, two heading directly upstairs, two fanning through the ground floor and back yard and two to the basement, according to their previous assignments.

Rory Biesu stood at the head of the staircase in a terry-towel bathrobe. "What the fuck is going on?"

"We have a warrant to search the premises, Mr. Biesu. Please come down and remain in the living room. Who else is in the house?" Desi said.

"Why the hell did you have to break down the door? I'm calling my lawyer."

"Who else is in the house, Mr. Biesu?" she repeated.

"No one."

"No assistant or other employee? The one who answered the phone the other day?"

He glared at her as he descended the staircase, cell phone already pressed to his ear.

"Not here."

She steered him into the living room.

"Where's the warrant?" Biesu barked. "I want to see the warrant. I'm going to sue you for damages."

"You're welcome to file a claim, Mr. Biesu," Desi said as she handed him the document.

Leaving a patrol officer to monitor Biesu, she wriggled her hands into Latex gloves and proceeded deeper into the mansion to oversee the search.

Fin had already gone ahead to check the basement where Flame had indicated the dungeon was located.

A door off the hall was ajar.

She peeked in and saw a staircase leading down. The light was on in the basement, and she could hear sounds of movement.

"Hey, McNab," she called as she walked down the steps.

"Come check this out," he called back.

The cellar had been converted into a lounge area decorated in a plush baroque style with tall candelabras, burgundy velvet upholstered couches and a wooden bar.

"Looks like a movie set for Dracula's castle," Desi said.

Fin pointed to the border of flames painted around the perimeter of the ceiling.

"Remind you of something?"

"I guess we've entered Thanatos," she said.

A doorway at the far end of the room was covered with a thick velvet curtain.

"Get a load of this." Fin beckoned for her to follow him.

They proceeded through the curtain into a hallway with four doors leading off it.

"This is where all the action takes place," he said.

Desi entered the first room.

It contained a massive wooden X with leather restraints at the end of each plank to tie a spread-eagled person.

Various instruments of torture hung from the walls: wooden paddles, riding crops, switches, maces, chains, and manacles. Metal hooks, nooses, and ropes hung from ceilings. A cop was bagging all the weapons.

"We're taking everything," Fin said.

"Jesus." Desi barely registered what he was saying. "This is a sex dungeon."

The other three rooms were similarly equipped with instruments designed to punish. One had stocks and a thumbscrew. Another had a hangman's noose and several black executioner's hoods.

The third had a body-shaped cage, like a mummy made of metal bands.

One of the uniforms straightened. "Found a propane torch and what looks like a poker for a fireplace."

Desi examined the tip of the metal rod. It looked about the diameter of a cigarette end. "Could this have made those burn marks on Parker's back?" she said.

"I'd say so," Fin said.

Desi handed it back to the officer with an instruction to bag it. "Let's find something we can charge him with," she announced in a loud voice. "There's got to be something here."

"Detective, I think I found it."

A young officer turned from a shelf of accessories. A pair of nunchucks dangled from his hand.

Desi grinned.

"Perfect. That's a felony possession charge right there. That'll make him squawk."

She left the dungeon and returned upstairs. The officers had gone through the kitchen, living room, and one was now searching Biesu's study, ransacking his desk drawers.

"Take all business receipts or documents," Desi said. "We have to prove he was running this dungeon thing as a business."

"What do you make of these?" The officer handed her a sheaf of papers.

Desi shuffled through them. They contained dozens of rows of number and letter strings.

"I don't know but let's take them."

Desi gave the papers back to the officer to bag and tag.

A tower of recordable DVDs rose from the floor of the study. She squatted and went through them. They were marked only with initials. "Take these, too," she said.

She proceeded upstairs. There were six bedrooms, including a palatial master suite the size of Desi's bungalow. It had a round bed draped with a gauzy curtain suspended from the ceiling. An officer was going through the contents of Biesu's walk-in closet, painstakingly searching jacket and pants pockets and the interior of shoes and tossing the searched garments onto the floor.

There had to be tens of thousands of dollars' worth of designer suits, shirts, and shoes lying in an unceremonious heap.

Desi checked the other bedrooms. One room seemed to be used for storage of old boxes, while three others were furnished with beds and dressers, but not occupied, judging by the bare mattresses.

The final room was the smallest and appeared to have been lived in but perhaps no longer. The place had been trashed. Sheets had been ripped from the bed and the mattress lay askew. Clothes and shoes, including thigh high black leather boots, were strewn everywhere.

The dresser had been stripped of its drawers, which were lying on the floor surrounded by hillocks of their contents—underwear and T-shirts. Makeup and toiletries appeared to have been swept onto the floor.

The door of the closet was slightly ajar. Desi pulled it fully open. Clothes hangers were empty except for a couple black leather harness outfits. Did one of the dommes live here? Why was the place such a mess?

She stepped backward onto the edge of a drawer lying apart from the others. It flipped up and bashed her on her calf muscle. In pain and annoyance, she heaved it aside. It landed upside down. Then she saw it. A small, plain white envelope taped to the underside. She ripped it off and opened it.

Desi pulled out a photo of two girls with flaxen hair, striking smiling poses for the camera. One was bigger than the other. She looked maybe twelve, while the other displayed the gappy smile of a five or six-year-old who had lost a front tooth.

Desi studied the background. The girls were sitting on a stone wall with a long-grassed field behind them and a row of pine trees in the distance and beyond them, the outline of hills.

Judging by the wall of closely fitted, unmortared stones, it looked like Europe.

She flipped it over. Nothing was written on the back. Why go to such lengths to hide a childhood photo? Was this what whoever had been searching for?

She slipped the picture back in the envelope and the envelope into an evidence baggie she drew from her pocket.

Desi trotted down the stairs and wheeled into the living room where Biesu was sitting on the couch with his legs crossed, one of them jouncing wildly.

"Mr. Biesu, who occupies that bedroom upstairs?"

"Which room?"

Desi rolled her eyes. "The only one besides yours that's occupied."

"Detective, although I have nothing to hide and I would love to satisfy your thirst for knowledge, my lawyer told me not to answer any of your questions unless she was present."

"You'd better call her to meet you at the station then. We're going to be booking you on a felony weapons charge, possession of nunchucks."

His smarminess dropped like an anchor. "What?"

Desi's phone chirped. She looked at the number. It was from downtown, the police administration building, which could mean nothing good. She moved into the hall, leaving Biesu to consider his fate, and clicked answer.

She stated her name in an official tone. It was a media relations officer, Heidi Fritz.

"We got a call from a reporter who says she was tipped off about a body found in a West LA alley, a victim of violent sex play," the media relations officer said.

Desi sighed. "Yeah, that's my case. I was really hoping it wouldn't make the press."

"We gotta release this stuff," Fritz said.

"I know. Just don't release too much, like cause of death or anything. Make it as sketchy as possible."

"Roger that."

Desi hung up. Shit. That was all she needed. A lawyer who died of masochistic sex games made a lurid story. Once it appeared in the Times, it would get picked up not only by other media, but by the brass, as well.

Her phone rang again. This time it was from a number she didn't recognize. She answered.

"Detective Nimmo? It's Cara Franceschi, Rory Biesu's neighbor. Are you there right now?"

The nosey neighbor wanted to know what was going on. Jesus. "Yes, Ms. Franceschi, I'm here and very busy. What can I do for you?"

"My maid says this girl who was working for Biesu has gone missing." Desi froze. "It's probably nothing but she's been worried about her. She's kind of been like a mother figure to her. When I saw the police cars go in, I thought maybe something happened."

"I'd like to talk to your maid," Desi said.

"She's here."

"Don't let her go anywhere. I'll be over as soon as I can."

Desi pocketed the phone, deep in thought. The trashed bedroom. Biesu's evasiveness. And now a missing woman.

13

"Desi." Fin beckoned her to come down the hall to meet him. "We found a closet downstairs with a bunch of recording equipment. It was wired up to cameras hidden in the dungeon walls. Biesu's been taping the S&M sessions."

Desi's eyes widened.

"There was a bunch of recordable DVDs in the study, marked with initials."

They looked at each other. "Sterling Parker may be on one of them," Fin said.

"That's what I'm thinking. Any branding irons?"

"No. We're almost done. I called for a truck to come and take the larger torture instruments directly down to the lab. If we find Parker's DNA on any of them, we got the asshole nailed."

"I just got a call from media relations. The Times got tipped off about Parker's body being found."

"Shit. I bet it was one of those women in the café," Fin said. "They seemed kind of excited about the whole thing."

"It was bound to happen sooner or later. I'd just prefer it was later. Fuck."

"It could help us," Fin said.

"I doubt it. I need to go next door. The maid is saying a girl who lived here is missing. There's a bedroom upstairs that's been ransacked, but Biesu was cagey when I asked him who lived there. This case might be bigger than we thought."

An officer carrying an evidence box approached. They squeezed to the side to let him pass.

"Somehow it doesn't surprise me," Fin said. "At any rate, I think we've got him on Parker, and maybe more, like extortion with the tapes."

Fin returned to the basement, and Desi instructed a patrol officer to take Biesu down to the station and told her she'd be following. Then she strode down the driveway and pressed the intercom at the Franceschis' gate.

It swung open immediately. She walked up to a sprawling, ranch house at the end of a curving drive. A kneeling gardener wearing a wide-brimmed straw hat plucked weeds out of a rose bed that bordered the home.

Cara Franceschi appeared from around the corner of the house and led her into the den. As soon as Desi saw photos on a wall, she knew why Cara looked vaguely familiar. She was the child star of a sixties TV show about a vet's daughter who could talk to animals. She'd played the daughter.

"I used to watch re-runs of your show when I was a kid," Desi said.

"I tried to get them to do a reboot with me playing a vet, but it was no go. Animal shows are a pain in the neck these days, all those PETA activists."

"Too bad. It was a good show."

"I still get residuals so I can't complain."

A woman in a pastel pink maid's uniform, her frizzy greying hair held back with a headband, entered, a nervous look in her eyes.

"This is Flavia," Cara said. "She's worked for me for years. She wants to talk to you about her friend." She nudged Flavia into an armchair across from Desi. The woman sat on it with a stiff back.

"Where are you from, Flavia?" Desi said.

"Brazil."

"I went to Carnaval in Rio once. It's a beautiful city, very warm people." It was a lie. Desi had never visited Brazil, but immigrants loved being told how nice their home country was. The story served its purpose. Flavia smiled and relaxed slightly. "What do you have to tell me?"

"My friend, she works for Mr. Biesu next door, she's missing."

"Why do you think she's missing?"

"She not answering my phone calls. She always answer my calls. And I went over there and she not there. The maid tell me she left, just like that. She not tell anybody. She wouldn't leave without telling me, I know she wouldn't."

"What's her name?"

"Dorina."

"You know her last name?"

She shook her head. "She tell me but I don't remember. We meet through a hole in the hedge between the houses. She come over when Mr. Biesu is asleep or out and we talk. He takes a lot of drugs and sleeping pills. When he's asleep, she sneak out. That's how I know something is wrong. She comes through the hole in the hedge, and I let her out of the gate, so she is not on Mr. Biesu's security camera. She never leave through my gate."

"She's also from Brazil?"

"A country in Europe. I don't know the name. She come here to work for Mr. Biesu. She does a lot of strange things, sex things, for him and his guests. Mr. Biesu is a bad man. One time she have bruises." She pointed to her wrists. "I tell her to get away from him."

"Maybe she did get away."

"I have a bad feeling. Last time I talk to her, she was scared of Mr. Biesu."

"Why? Why was she scared?"

"She not tell me. She say she didn't want to involve me."

"When was the last time you saw her?"

"Four days ago." The day of Sterling Parker's death.

"You said she came here to work for him. She knew him from before, in her country?"

"She know him through her sister."

The photo of the two girls. Desi took it out of her pocket and showed it to Flavia. "Is this her and her sister?"

Flavia studied it but her face remained a frown. "Maybe. But Dorina has black hair now." She handed back the picture and fished out a cheap cell phone from her apron pocket. "I have photo of her."

She handed Desi the phone. It displayed a texted selfie of a waif-like woman with watery blue eyes, the paleness of her skin in stark relief to the darkness of her hair. It very well could have been dyed. She stood under the curl of a man's muscular arm.

"Can I text this photo to myself? It might be important," Desi said. Flavia nodded.

Desi thumbed in her phone number, pressed send and returned the phone to Flavia.

"So maybe Dorina is with her sister. Do you know her name?"

Flavia shook her head. "Dorina cannot find her sister. She come here to find her."

"The sister was working for Mr. Biesu then left and never contacted Dorina?"

"Yes, that is right. So Dorina contact Mr. Biesu."

Could Dorina be Mistress Odyne, the other dominatrix? "Is Dorina working off her debt to Mr. Biesu for bringing her here?"

"I think, yes, something like that, but she has a lawyer helping her to get papers."

The immigration law book on Sterling Parker's dining room table. Desi felt disparate pieces snapping together like a jigsaw puzzle. He'd been helping Dorina legalize her status.

"Do you know the name of the lawyer?"

She shook her head.

"How did she meet him?"

"He comes to Mr. Biesu's parties. He like her, feel sorry for her."

"Romania, was that where she was from?"

"No, I never hear of her country. She say it is very small and poor."

"How old is Dorina?"

"Nineteen. She is like my daughter. You will find her?"

"I'll do my best. You contact me if anything else comes up, okay?" Desi gave her a business card, which she took with a solemn face.

Desi's plain wrap was the only cop car left at Biesu's mansion, which now stood in silence. It was odd that Fin hadn't even texted her that they were clearing the scene.

Before hitting the station, she headed down Wilshire Boulevard. She had a pitstop to make.

Desi entered the Pen & Ink Café, which was full of hipsters huddled over laptops, and spotted Pigtails behind the counter.

The barista smiled cautiously, the prickles of their last exchange still remembered.

"Detective, you here for a coffee or on business?"

"Business, but I'll take a latte."

"You got it."

"Adriana around?"

"She's on her break. Go on in the back." Pigtails held up the counter door so Desi could enter, then turned to fixing the coffee.

The barista was sitting at a table eating a salad and reading something on her phone propped against a saltshaker.

"That reminds me, I never ate lunch," Desi said.

Adriana looked up with a start. "Detective, what brings you by? Any news on that guy?"

"Making progress. I wanted to show you something."

She took out her phone, scrolled to Flavia's picture of Dorina and slid it in front of Adriana. She wiped her hands on her apron before taking it.

"Is that the girl you saw in here that night with Sterling Parker?"

Adriana squinted at it. "You know, could be. It kind of looks like her."

"Can you be more definite?"

"I really only saw her from the back, but the hair looks the right color."

Desi took back the phone. "Thanks," she said. "It was a long shot, but you never know."

"Sorry," Adriana said. "Hope you find her."

"We're close. By the way, have you or your boss spoken to anyone from the media about this?"

Adriana looked at her blankly. "No. Is it true that the guy died of injuries in some S&M sex thingy? That's what the paper said."

"It's already in the newspaper?"

"On the website. Just posted. See? It's really short but mentions the café."

Adriana handed Desi her phone. The article quoted an anonymous source close to the investigation saying the victim "was believed to have died during a violent sex ritual."

Shit. Where had the reporter gotten that? It wasn't the baristas. They had never known anything about Parker's wounds or cause of death. She handed back the phone.

"If you do get approached by the media, it would be a big help if you didn't say anything. We're actively working the investigation. Any details made public could really hurt us," Desi said.

"Sure, no problem," Adriana said. "Anything to help."

Desi returned to the front of the café, where her latte was waiting. She paid, then stuffed the change in the tip jar and took her coffee outside. As she stood on the sidewalk sipping it, the afternoon sun bounced off the concrete into her eyes.

Who the fuck had called the newspaper?

14

Desi was climbing the stairs to the squad room when Lt. Butler poked her head out of her office. "Desi, come on in for a minute."
Did she have some kind of antenna that signaled when Desi was arriving? She probably wanted an update on case status.

Butler sat back in her chair behind her desk. "I noticed McNab came in solo from doing the search. He said you're investigating a report of a missing girl and some sort of abuse in porn movies?"

Desi felt a rise of anger. What the hell had he said that to the LT for? He should've let her tell the lieutenant.

"There's something else going on here. I think Parker is only the tip of it. We found a camera system set up in the dungeon rooms and a bunch of DVDs. Biesu's been recording the S&M sessions, maybe for extortion, I don't know. There's other stuff too: a missing woman, possibly two, and some indication of a sex trafficking scheme. The people involved aren't saying anything. I don't know exactly what it is, but I have a hunch that Biesu is at the center of a lot of shit."

Butler slapped her palm on the desk. "I don't want time wasted on hunches. If there's credible evidence, turn it over to the appropriate unit downtown. They can investigate. We need to focus on quality-of-life crime committed in our jurisdiction. That's our job."

"I know, LT, but I do have …"

"By the way, Biesu's lawyer is on his way. She's raising a stink about her client being taken into custody."

"We found nunchucks in the toss."

"According to the lawyer, Biesu was a martial arts instructor."

Desi was stunned. That was the only loophole for legally owning nunchucks. Biesu wouldn't talk now.

She shook her head in disbelief. "No way."

"The lawyer's bringing proof. If it checks, we gotta kick him. She's talking about suing for damages for the gate and front door, plus the cost of security until the gate is replaced."

"Are we going to let him walk? Biesu's not going to talk without something on him."

"This BD-whatever stuff isn't illegal, and we have nothing so far that shows Biesu's direct involvement in Parker's death. From what McNab tells me, it likely wasn't Biesu who administered the fatal injury to Parker. We've still got forensics to come from on all the stuff from the sex dungeon. I've asked McNab to keep me updated."

"If that stuff was used on multiple people, I don't know what kind of DNA sample they can get from it. Plus, it was the brand that killed him, not handcuffs, and we didn't find any brands."

"One step at a time, Desi. McNab said he's got a line on where the brand might be located and he's still waiting for one manufacturer to report back."

McNab, McNab, McNab. The investigation was suddenly pivoting around McNab. Butler must've had a real heart-to-heart with the guy. Desi needed to assert her role.

"By the way, I've located the witness who was with Parker the night of his death, but she appears to be missing," she said.

The lieutenant looked dubious. "You didn't really locate her then."

"I ascertained her identity. I think she's a possible trafficking victim. It's a matter of time before I find her."

"Time is in short supply. Get back to it, then. But stay focused on the homicide."

Desi left and entered the squad room, looking for her so-called partner. Somehow she felt played, that she never should have trusted him. But what the hell had she been supposed to do? She had to work with the guy.

She stopped at Keisha Hardy's desk. "You seen McNab?" she asked.

"He was floating around here somewhere," she said, studying her colleague. "Anything wrong?"

"You were right, that's what's wrong."

Desi passed McNab's desk. It was still scattered with Sterling Parker's DVDs. He wasn't sticking to the rules about handling evidence. Should she run into the Butler and return the tattle-telling favor?

She paused. The DVDs. Something about them nagged her still.

She picked one up, hoping it would pry loose whatever it was tugging at the back of her brain.

"McNab's in an interview room, if you're looking for him," Diego Jauregui called from his desk.

"I am." She dropped the DVD and walked down the hall, meeting Fin on his way out.

"Where the fuck have you been?" he said.

"Nice to see you, too." Desi crossed her arms and stood in the middle of the passage. "I've been interviewing a witness."

"Biesu's lawyer is downstairs. I'm about to bring her up."

"Why the fuck did you run your mouth off about me to the LT?"

"She asked where you were and what was going on. I told her," Fin said.

"Couldn't you have waited?" Desi said.

"Can we do this later?" He moved to skirt her, but she stepped to the side and blocked him. "Come on, Desi."

She leaned into his face. "If you don't have my back, I sure as fuck won't have yours. See you in there, *partner*."

She moved aside to let Fin pass, then returned to the squad room to gather a pad and pen. It was becoming obvious what McNab was doing. He wanted her off the case so he could have it to himself. Well, she was damned if she was going to let that happen. Not when she was this deep into it.

When the case was over, she'd go to Butler and request a new partner. The only problem was that Fin, for some reason, seemed to have gained the LT's favor. The risk of asking for a partner switch would be that Fin would end up with top slot of major crimes, and she, Desi, would end up with second billing.

She had never had a big ego, but she didn't know if she could take being pushed aside for the second time in her career. She had to clear her head, get ready for Biesu.

She strode into the interview room, where Biesu was drumming a tattoo on the table with his free hand. The other was handcuffed to a steel ring in the table's center next to a plastic cup of water.

Biesu glared at her as she entered.

"Your lawyer will be right up, Mr. Biesu. Can I get you more water?"

He answered with a scowl.

"I'll take that as a no."

As Desi pulled out a chair, the door opened. Fin entered followed by a slim, silver-haired woman in a double-breasted trouser suit and carrying a briefcase. She set it on the table and snapped it open, removing a yellow legal pad and a silver pen.

"May I have a moment with my client?"

The detectives stood at the door while the attorney and Biesu huddled.

Fin glanced at the woman. "Is she costing him four hundred an hour? What do you think?" he said.

He was trying to make nice. She glared at him.

"You want to lead?" he continued.

"You're always the good cop, right?" she said in a sharp tone.

The attorney signaled they were ready. She announced her name as Charlotte Specchio and rattled off the multiple names of a downtown LA law firm.

"Mr. Biesu, we're investigating the death of Sterling Parker due to injuries sustained at your club Thanatos," Fin said.

Specchio jumped in. "My client has already answered your questions about Mr. Parker and has told you he did not know him personally. You have no proof that Mr. Parker's injuries, whatever they may be, were sustained at his residence or that he had anything to do with those injuries."

"We have witnesses, Ms. Specchio," Desi said.

"I reiterate, my client has already answered those questions. My client was arrested for possession of an illegal weapon, which I can prove was in his possession legally." She took out a paper and slid it across the table at the detectives.

It was a computer printout from the World Karate Association website listing Rory Biesu as a recipient of a black belt in karate and a certified instructor.

"We'll have to verify this with the World Karate Association," Fin said.

"Of course," Specchio said. "Go right ahead."

"Why were the nunchucks in Mr. Biesu's sex dungeon?" Desi said. "Surely, Mr. Biesu knows they're a dangerous weapon."

"He does not know how they ended up there and admits it was an error. There are other people in his home at times, and we assume that one of them came across the nunchucks, did not know what they were, and assuming they were a part of the paraphernalia, wrongly placed them with the other items."

"Does Mr. Biesu own any branding irons?" Fin asked.

"No, he does not."

"Does Mr. Biesu have a license for operating an entertainment venue?" Desi said.

"He does not because he doesn't operate an entertainment venue. He hosts social gatherings, parties."

"Where people get beaten, whipped, handcuffed, chained, and burned," Fin shot back.

"Because they are adherents to a particular lifestyle, which is not illegal. Do you have any complaints, any victims?"

"We have a dead man," Desi said.

"As stated, Mr. Biesu has nothing to do with that."

"Mr. Biesu, who is Mistress Odyne?" Desi looked directly at him.

Specchio leaned into him, and he whispered in her ear. She nodded. "She's a guest at Mr. Biesu's social events," she said.

"Can Mr. Biesu answer the question directly?" Desi said.

"She's a guest at my social events," Biesu parroted.

"Does she live with Mr. Biesu in his mansion?"

They conferred again. "I maintain rooms for any guest who feels they cannot drive home or is in need of a place to stay," he said.

"What is Mistress Odyne's real name?"

Another whispered conference. "I don't remember offhand."

"Where is Mistress Odyne, Mr. Biesu?"

For the first time, he spoke without consulting his lawyer. "I don't know."

Fin gave Desi a meaningful look. He wanted to get some questions in.

"We found camera equipment hidden in the rooms in the basement. What is that used for?" he said.

Biesu leaned into Specchio. They exchanged whispers. "Sometimes guests want a record of their sessions," he said.

"You're saying it's only used at their request and with their full knowledge?"

"Yes."

"Why hide the camera then?"

"So they don't feel self-conscious."

Fin looked at Desi and tilted his head to the side.

"One moment please."

The detectives crossed to the door. "You got anything else?" he said.

"I have plenty else, but I don't want to tip my hand just yet. You?" she said.

"We're not going to get anywhere with this bulldog, not until we get something hard on him," he said.

Desi nodded and the detectives approached the table.

"That'll be all for now, Mr. Biesu," Fin said. "But we may need to speak to you again."

"I assume my client is free to go?"

"For now. If we find this certification is false, we will issue an arrest warrant," he said.

The attorney stood. "I'll also be pursuing compensation for the broken gate and door."

"That's entirely your prerogative," Fin said.

The detectives walked wordlessly back to the squad room.

Fin peeled off to the break room while Desi went to her desk. She couldn't help thinking they were missing something and that she was playing catchup to McNab. If there was a time that she needed her old partner, Sam Burkehalter, it was now.

She still missed his counsel, as well as his dry wit delivered in the slight drawl of a rural Indiana upbringing. He'd tell her what to do about McNab and where to go in the case.

She closed her eyes. What would Sam do?

"Follow the money," sprang into her head. It had been one of Sam's mantras.

When it came to rich people and crime, answers often lay at the end of a financial trail, or at the very least along the way. And, unlike poor people's money, rich people's money left a Hansel-and-Gretel path of crumbs to follow. The problem was finding it, and Desi wasn't finding Rory Biesu's.

Biesu likely charged his Thanatos clients a pricey amount to indulge in their proclivities, but Desi couldn't see it generating millions of dollars. The same with a couple of low-budget porn flicks.

Cara Franceschi had mentioned a cryptocurrency. He could've boosted his net worth on a couple substantial overnight trading plays. Whatever he was up to, Desi was sure there was some illegal aspect to it. The guy oozed sliminess.

She opened her top desk drawer and pulled out a stack of business cards she'd collected over the years. She rifled through until she found the one she was looking for and typed an email.

"Buy you a late lunch across the street?" Fin said as he returned to his work station.

Desi studied him. He was trying to make it up to her. It really didn't make sense to refuse. She still had to work with the guy, but she would no longer trust him. "You're on."

As they walked to the cafe, Fin offered his apology.

"Listen, I'm sorry about Butler. She asked where you were and ..." He shrugged.

"I appreciate the apology, but in the future, just say I'm in the field and leave it at that. Everything else is on a need-to-know basis. Brass doesn't need to know everything all the time."

"Absolutely," Fin said.

"Another thing. Stop trying to undermine me. You've been at it since the get-go. Just stop, okay?"

Fin stared at her. "Sorry if you feel ..."

She cut him off. "Cut the bullshit. I know what you're trying to do."

Desi yanked open the door of the restaurant and they entered. The place was covered in fifties' movie posters and LP covers. They sat at a vinyl booth and studied the menu amid an awkward silence. After ordering sandwiches, Fin sat back.

"What did you get from the neighbor?" he said. He was letting her accusation go.

She filled him in on what Flavia had told her, and then weighed whether she should tell him about the photo of Dorina and her sister, which was still in her jacket pocket. She decided against it.

She hadn't recorded it as an item taken in the search, and given Fin's track record so far, she didn't need to give her partner ammunition against her.

"I think Dorina was the woman with Parker the night he died," Desi said. "Biesu had searched her room, looking for something. She got scared and called Parker for help. He'd been helping her with her immigration stuff, so she figured he was a lawyer, he'd know what to do about whatever it was.

"Unfortunately, he was close to dying. When he croaked, she took off. She couldn't go back to Biesu's."

"If Dorina is illegal, that could explain why she didn't help him when he took ill. She was scared of cops or anyone else arriving on the scene," Fin said. "But where the hell could she have gone?"

The waitress arrived with a chicken salad sandwich for Desi and a club for Fin.

"The million-dollar question," Desi said. "It doesn't sound as if Dorina had many people to turn to. Flavia, the next-door maid, was too close to Biesu's place."

Desi bit into her sandwich as Fin reached for the ketchup.

"You're putting ketchup on a club sandwich?"

"Yeah, what's wrong with that?"

Desi scrunched her face. "Hey, whatever trips your tastebuds."

"Dorina could've branded Sterling Parker, you know," Fin said through a mouthful.

Desi nodded as she chewed.

"She's a suspect as well as a witness. We have to find her. She's probably knows everything going on at that mansion. I think she was holding back from the maid, maybe out of embarrassment, shame, or just to protect her. Bryony Podeswa is our answer."

"She's going to be tough," Fin said.

"We get tough with her. We bring her in."

"What if Parker wasn't branded at Thanatos? Could be some other place," Fin said. "We need to bring in Steve Wu, press him on other dommes or other dungeon places."

"So far we've found nothing indicating Sterling was going to another place. My money's on Biesu."

Desi's cell phone rang. She recognized the number as media relations.

Now what? She picked up.

"Officer Heidi Fritz. We're getting a shitload of calls from the press about this Parker case. Is there anything else we can release at this time?"

"Nope. The investigation is ongoing, period."

"Roger."

Desi hung up. "Media relations. Everybody in the press is all over this story now. They're calling for progress updates and details."

"Shit," Fin said.

"It wasn't the baristas at that café who leaked it. They didn't know about the BDSM angle because we didn't know about it when we talked to them." She eyed him carefully as she spoke.

He took a bite of his sandwich and chewed. "They always seem to find out stuff, don't they?" he said, looking at his plate.

15

Fin was close to breaking open the Sterling Parker homicide. He could feel it. He looked at himself in the mirror as he washed his hands. He also had the lieutenant on his side. Desi going off to the neighbor's and leaving him to return alone to the squad room had been a gift that he had quickly unwrapped with a stop in Butler's office. He updated her on the search and had managed to slip in the tidbit of information that Desi was off investigating some tangent, accompanying it with a dubious hike of his eyebrows.

Butler had stared at him with a frown, and then to his surprise had censured Desi.

He really hadn't wanted her to do that. He would've preferred that she kept the information to herself so as not to alert Desi to stay on the reservation. The more she moved off it, the better for him.

Plus, he'd had to backpedal to regain her good graces. She was wary of him now, so he'd have to play things carefully. Nevertheless, he had accomplished his goal, which was to gain the eyes and ears of the brass and impress them with his single-minded focus on solving the case. That was what mattered, not being best buds with a two-bit detective whose career had hit a dead-end.

She had seemed a little suspicious about the newspaper leak, but he thought he'd played it off well. She'd seemed satisfied with his response.

He dried his hands with paper towels and headed upstairs feeling the cell phone vibrate in his back pocket. Incoming emails.

Reading through them as he ambled to his desk, he felt the jab of electric current and picked up his pace, climbing the stairs two at a time.

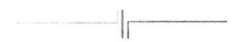

Back in the squad room, Desi walked past Fin's desk, again noticing the DVDs. He was still downstairs. She picked up "The Blood Room."

Then she saw it.

She pulled out her cell phone, calling up the picture of Dorina that Flavia had sent her, enlarging the arm dangling around her shoulder.

A tattoo decorated the inside of a bicep. A five-pointed star inside a circle. A pentacle, a symbol of witchcraft. She looked at the DVD cover featuring Flame and squinted at his raised arm holding the poker.

She could just make out the five points of a star-shaped mark within the outline of a circle. She looked at the skin tone.

The same honey color. She lowered the DVD.

What was Flame doing with Dorina?

She put the DVD back, went to her desk and started checking her inbox.

"Just got an email from Steve Wu's lawyer," Fin said. Desi swiveled in her chair. "He's bringing him in this afternoon for the interview."

"Great, but I don't think we'll get much out of him."

"And even better, we got the brand. The brand manufacturer in Texas says they filled an order two and a half years ago for that symbol and shipped it to a Barbara Powell, address in LA. Who the hell could that be?"

Desi thought for a moment.

"BP, Bryony Podeswa. Does the address match what we got on her?"

"No."

"Hold on." Desi swiveled back to her computer and called up Podeswa's DMV records. "What's the street?"

"South Alma."

Desi scrolled down previous addresses. "Here it is. It's her." She met Fin's eyes. "Up for another toss? You're writing this one."

The way to deal with ego-driven colleagues like Finbar McNab was simple: be a bitch or they didn't respect you. Forget about being liked. Desi didn't know why she'd even bothered giving him the benefit of the doubt and trying to get along with him.

Her first impression of him had been on the mark and that had been underlined by his brown-nosing of the LT. She wasn't going to cut Finbar McNab any more slack, nor was she going to keep him completely informed as to what she was doing.

She left him writing up the search warrant for Bryony Podeswa and headed over to the UCLA campus in nearby Westwood and found the Anderson School of Business and the office of Sheila Prosser, finance professor.

"Come in," a woman's voice sang.

Desi entered as Sheila was removing a pile of hefty books from the chair in front of her desk.

"I review books for a business journal, so I get tons of them," she said in an Australian accent. "More than I could possibly hope to review."

Desi looked around the office where stacks of books were piled high. "What do you do with them all?"

"Donate some to the library, put some out as giveaways for staff and students. They're pretty dry business books so people aren't exactly keen to pick them up. Have a seat, Detective."

"Any on cryptocurrencies?" Desi sat in the chair that the professor had just cleared off.

Prosser smiled and pushed a strand of loose hair behind an ear as she sat behind her messy desk. "I'm writing that one. If I can make the publisher's deadline and that's a big if."

"The one I'm interested in is called 'monero.' Have you heard of that one?"

"Sure. It's like bitcoin but with an important difference. It obscures the details of the transaction. The sender, receiver, and the amount being exchanged are all secret. With bitcoin, there's a registry that records the transactions so they're traceable, contrary to popular belief."

"How does monero obscure the transaction exactly?"

"Each individual transaction is coded with a unique string of numbers and letters that serves as its shield. Sort of like a Swiss numbered bank account."

Strings of numbers and letters. The sheaf of pages in Biesu's desk.

"Do you have an example of what a transaction code looks like by any chance?"

"As a matter of fact, I do. I'm writing a chapter on this model of cryptocurrency." Prosser turned to her laptop, typed and then turned the screen to face Desi. She leaned forward to examine the page displayed on the computer.

The examples of monero transactions looked just like the ones on Biesu's documents.

Desi sat back. "Why would someone be making a couple hundred monero transactions?"

Prosser gave a small shrug. "Investment or trading, in other words, buying or selling something. Speculators hold on to cryptocurrencies hoping their value increases and then sell, or some people buy something with it as with any other currency. The seller can convert the proceeds into a more readily used currency, such as bitcoin or US dollars, for that matter."

"And this can be anywhere in the world," Desi said.

"Anywhere. I should add the transfers are instant. You don't have to wait for your monero."

"Could someone become extremely rich off monero?"

"There are quite a few cryptocurrency multimillionaires around."

"How could someone trace income or revenue from monero transactions?"

"It could be hard if it's laundered in any of the usual ways or it could be as simple as checking deposits in bank accounts."

Desi paused, processing the information as to how it might relate to Rory Biesu. She looked at Prosser. "If buyers and sellers and amounts are kept secret, monero would be a perfect way to buy and sell illegal items, like on the dark web."

"Not 'would,' Detective, it already is."

16

Bryony Podeswa put up no resistance when the detectives showed up with the warrant. She scanned it and let them in as if she'd been expecting them.

"Go ahead," she said. "I got nothing to hide." She sat on the grass, legs crossed, and lit a cigarette as if she were waiting for a bus.

Her cottage was a dimly lit, single room with a kitchenette and a small bathroom housed behind a plastic shower curtain. A curtain covered the sole small window situated high on a wall. The place smelled thick and rank like bed linen long in need of a wash.

Spotting the drop ceiling, Fin immediately stood on a chair and started pushing up the panels supported by a light aluminum frame. He systematically went panel by panel. Nothing. He pulled apart the bed, tossing the sheets and cover onto the floor, then heaving up the mattress.

A roller suitcase lay under the bed. He pulled it out. It was full of BDSM toys. He spotted the end of an iron rod and tugged it out from under the pile. The rod ended in an oval with a horizontal line across the center.

"Bingo," he announced. Triumph shone on his face.

Desi turned from searching the kitchen cabinets. "Let's take her in," she said.

Fin dashed outside. Bryony's face dropped when she saw the iron rod in his hand. Her arm jerked as she drew the cigarette to her lips and took a deep puff. She said nothing.

"Ms. Podeswa, you're going to have to come down to the station," Fin said.

She flicked the cigarette onto the driveway and exhaling a jet of smoke, unfolded her legs and stood.

"We've got some questions about this brand, Bryony," Fin said, parking a haunch on the table in the station interview room where Podeswa was slumped in a chair with a dark look across her eyes.

"I want to call my lawyer," she said in a flat tone, avoiding his eyes.

"Who's your lawyer?"

"Charlotte Specchio." Fin exchanged a glance with Desi, who was leaning against a wall, arms crossed.

"Sure, you can call your lawyer," Fin said. "You can wait in the holding cell 'til she comes."

The request for an attorney effectively ended the interview before it started. The detectives left the room.

"Biesu's lawyer. Fuck, I should've guessed," Fin said as they walked down the hall.

"Biesu's probably footing her legal bill, too. I don't think Bryony could afford a white-shoe like Specchio." Desi tossed her pad on her keyboard. "We can hold her for forty-eight hours. See if that will loosen her up."

Desi gathered her purse and the keys to the plain wrap.

"Steve Wu is coming in with his lawyer, remember?" Fin said.

"You can handle."

"Where are you going?"

"To find our missing wit." She pivoted and exited the squad room before Fin had a chance to speak.

Where the hell was Desi going?

Steve Wu and his attorney Jack Steinberg looked like they'd consulted on their wardrobe before arriving at the police station.

Each had on a navy blue suit, a red tie, and a triangle of dazzling white handkerchief poking out of the breast pocket of his suit jacket.

Steinberg pushed his business card across the table at Fin. "My client is here purely in the spirit of cooperation. He admits no culpability in the death of Mr. Parker or anything else."

Fin let the card sit on the table. "Understood, and we appreciate your cooperation." He addressed Steve Wu. "Do you belong to a private BDSM club called Thanatos?"

Wu licked his lips. "Yes."

"Did you refer Sterling Parker to this club?"

Wu's eyes darted to his attorney, who jumped in. "Mr. Wu is not going to answer any questions regarding Mr. Parker. Mr. Wu was acquainted with Mr. Parker and that's all we're prepared to say at this time. Next question."

"Is Thanatos located at the residence of Rory Biesu?"

"Yes."

"Did you at any time see branding irons on the premises?"

"No."

"Did you hear of anyone being branded or burnt?"

"No."

Steinberg had coached his client well. The interview proceeded with Wu's mostly negative monosyllabic answers to Fin's questions. If a potential answer to a question seemed to steer into anything incriminating, the lawyer would place a gentle hand on Wu's forearm and say, "Next question, Detective."

After thirty-three minutes, Fin gave up. 'I think that about does it, Mr. Wu. We may need to talk to you at a later date, so we'd appreciate it if you stick around town."

Steinberg stood, buttoning his jacket. "You have my card, Detective. Just call and make an appointment."

Fin squeezed out a smile. He had got nothing from Steve Wu. He returned to the squad room and dropped in his chair, throwing his pen onto the desk. The thing that peeved him most of all wasn't Steinberg. It was the fact that Desi had been right. That was why she'd left him to deal with Wu. Where the fuck was she anyway?

A purpled twilight was crushing the remnants of the day by the time Desi reached San Fernando. She turned down Flame's street. Shaggy-haired teenagers skateboarded down the sidewalk. Girls sat like pigeons along the curb watching them.

Desi knocked on the door of the apartment, noting that the blinds in the front windows were closely drawn. "Flame, open up," she commanded. No answer.

She strode around the side of the house, bending to peer through windows in the gap where the blinds didn't quite meet the sills, but it was dark inside. As she rounded the corner of the house into the backyard, a leg rolled over the rear wooden fence.

"Police! Freeze!" Desi shouted. The leg disappeared. "Shit!"

She threw herself into a sprint. Using the old bicycle leaning against the fence that Flame must have used to boost himself over, she did the same. She hiked a leg over the fence top and flipped herself over as the bicycle slipped under her weight.

She thudded onto a backyard lawn, feeling pain shoot through her heels into her legs, pulled herself up and saw a path down the right side of the house. She launched into a canter, emerging onto the front lawn. Flame was speeding down the sidewalk. She threw herself into overdrive, but he had a good lead on her.

A woman was pushing a stroller ahead of him, clueless to the chase happening behind her. Flame shoved her to the side, knocking her and the stroller into a small hedge. Desi cast a glance at them as she galloped by. They looked okay. She kept going.

A gardener was staring wide-eyed at the pursuit as he watered a bed of succulents along the strip between the street and sidewalk.

"Police! Stop him!" Desi yelled.

The old man grabbed the hose snaking across the pavement and pulled it taut just as Flame flew by. The hose caught him on the shin, and he tripped, thudding to the sidewalk on his chin. He made to get up, but the gardener directed the hose nozzle at the back of his head, forcing him back to the sidewalk.

Catching up to her quarry, Desi knelt and pressed a knee to the middle of his back as she whipped out handcuffs. She yanked back his wrists and snapped them into steel bracelets.

"Thank you, sir," she said.

The old man nodded. He didn't seem to speak English. She grabbed one of Flame's arms and yanked him to his feet. Water dripped down his face. He shook his head, spraying water like a dog.

"Now Flame, you're going to tell me all about Dorina."

Flame pulled his wet, quilled arms tighter against his body. His grazed chin was dotted with blood from his crash landing. Desi marched him to the car and pushed him into the back seat.

"Look, I didn't do nothing wrong," he protested. "I don't even know why I'm sitting here. I need medical attention."

"You're here because you fled the police and ignored instructions to halt. Now I can take you down to the station and book you for obstruction or you can tell me what I need to know. The whole truth this time." He was silent. "What's your relationship with Dorina?"

Recognition flashed in his eyes, but he said nothing.

"Flame, you're in deep shit here of your own doing. You help me, I'll help you."

"I ain't got nothing to do with her or whatever she's mixed up in, and that's the truth," he said.

"Let's start at the beginning," Desi coaxed.

He sighed. "Dorina called me up a few days ago out of the blue. I ain't seen her for a while. We got friendly when I was working at the mansion then Biesu got wind of it and told me to stay away from her or I'd regret it. I guess he laid dibs on her. He's a nasty piece of work, got connections, know what I'm sayin'? No piece of ass is worth getting on his wrong side, so I distanced myself right quick. I found another gig."

"What night was this, that she called you?" Desi prompted.

He thought. "Wednesday. It was late, like ten-thirty. She said she needed a place to stay for a couple days. She sounded really out of it, like distraught. I said I didn't know. I was thinking of Biesu, but then she begged me and said she really needed help. I felt sorry for her, so I said okay. I went and picked her up in West LA near the 405 off ramp on Santa Monica Boulevard."

Right down the street from the Pen & Ink Café. The time, date, and place fit. Dorina was the woman with Sterling Parker the night he died.

"Did you ask Dorina what happened?" Desi said.

Flame shook his head. "Sometimes the less you know, the better. I judged this to be one of those times."

"She must've said something," Desi said.

Flame looked out the window. Desi followed his gaze. A kid riding a skateboard wiped out. He got up, grinning. "Biesu's a bad guy, Flame. I need your help to put him away."

"You ain't gonna charge me with nothing?"

"Not if you tell me the truth."

"Dorina said she was scared she was gonna end up like her sister."

"Why? What happened to her sister?" He said nothing and kept staring out the window. "Come on, Flame."

"She disappeared. She was working for Biesu then she like vanished. She never contacted Dorina. Dorina came here to try to find her. Dorina told me she found something that made her think Biesu had something to do with her disappearance."

"What do you mean?" Desi said.

"She didn't say, and I didn't ask. Like I said, there are some things you just don't want to know," Flame said.

The ransacked bedroom.

Biesu had been searching for something. Desi remembered the photo. The two sisters. She took it out from her jacket pocket and showed it to Flame.

"Yeah, that could be her and her sister except Dorina has black hair now. Ha, I never knew she dyed it. I thought that was her natural color."

"So Dorina's the younger one?"

"Yeah, like seven years younger. Her sister was like a mother to Dorina back in their country. She came here to make money to send back for Dorina. Dorina was living with an aunt because the parents were both dead, died in a car crash or something. The plan was for the sister to send for Dorina when she could, but she stopped contacting Dorina. As soon as Dorina was old enough, she came here to look for her."

"Is Dorina Mistress Odyne?"

"Yeah, that was her handle."

"And her sister?"

"She was working that dominatrix shit, too, back when Biesu was doing movies, not the club."

"Where was Dorina from?"

"Some place in Eastern Europe, some place I never heard of."

"Romania?"

"Nah, I heard of Romania. I would've remembered that."

Desi took out her phone and searched for a map of Eastern Europe. She started reading off names of countries.

"Serbia, Croatia, Macedonia, Bosnia and Herzegovina, Albania, Slovakia, Moldova, Bulgaria—"

"Wait, I think that was it."

"Bulgaria?"

"Before that."

"Moldova?"

"Yeah, that's it. Moldova. That's where she was from. I remember thinking what a weird name, like a moldy place. She only came like six months ago. She said she spent years learning English because it was her dream to come to America."

Desi thought. "Did Biesu bring the sister here before he brought Dorina?"

"Yeah, something like that. He was from a town near theirs. He said he could get them jobs here."

Biesu had said he was from Romania. Why did he lie? "Flame, where's Dorina now?"

"I don't know. The next day I went out and when I got back, she was gone. Tell you the truth, it was kind of a relief. She don't know many people here so if Biesu was looking for her, he might come straight to me. When you knocked at the door, I got scared. I knew you might be back about her. That's why I ran for it. That's everything I know, I swear. Are you going to drop the charge against me?"

Desi hadn't charged or been going to charge him with anything. "Yeah, I'm dropping everything." She got out and opened the rear door for Flame. "But the next time I come knocking, you answer, hear me?"

He got out and she unlocked his handcuffs. "Yes, ma'am," he said, rubbing his wrists.

Desi sat in the car for a minute. Moldova. She looked it up on her phone. It was a tiny country, sandwiched between Romania and Ukraine.

A former Soviet republic, formerly part of Romania. That could be why Biesu said he was Romanian. Being ethnic Romanian could have some higher social standing. Moldova was the least visited country in Europe and the poorest. In other words, Moldova was a place that people were desperate to escape from.

Desi lowered her phone. And now Dorina was desperate to escape from Biesu. What had made her so scared? She remembered the name on the paper she'd found in his car. Ruslana Ludmila Cojocaru. Was that Dorina's real name? What had happened to Dorina's sister? Even if the older sister had got away from Biesu, it seemed likely that she would've found some way to contact her younger sister, at least after waiting a while for things to cool off. It sounded like they had little more than each other in the world.

Desi looked around. This was a neighborhood where people were outside. Somebody must've seen Dorina leave. She probably didn't have much money. She could've left on foot.

There was only one way to find out. Desi got out of the car and walked to Flame's neighbor in the duplex and knocked on the door. No answer.

She tried a couple more doors on each side of Flame's unit, showing them the picture of Dorina on her phone. Nobody had seen her.

She left her card with the neighbors and returned to the Crown Vic.

She gulped down some water and started the engine. She was about to pull out when a minivan turned into the driveway belonging to the apartment next to Flame's.

A woman with curly hair and sunglasses got out, opened the back door, and leaned in to take something out of the rear seat.

Desi summoned a burst of energy and rolled out of the car. "Ma'am?" she called.

The woman straightened, looking around as she adjusted a roly-poly infant onto the crook of her hip. Desi identified herself and showed her the photo on her phone.

"I'm looking for anyone who might have seen this woman. She was staying with your downstairs neighbor three, four days ago. It's very important we find her," Desi said.

The woman peered over her sunglasses at Desi's phone. "I did see her," she said. "She and her friend made such a racket that it woke the baby."

"What happened?" Desi asked.

"Some woman was hammering on the door downstairs, yelling 'I know you're in there, Dora. Come out of there!' It was around ten in the morning. I know because the baby was due to sleep for another half-hour. I was pretty annoyed, so I looked out the window to see who it was, especially as two gay guys live there, and these were women's voices. I'd never seen either of them before."

"Did Dora come out?" Desi prompted.

"Eventually, yes. The woman banging on the door was saying, 'Nothing's going to happen to you. You'll be safe. I'll protect you'. It was a little weird."

"Can you describe the woman knocking?"

"I didn't get a look at her face, but she had long black hair. She was driving an old dark blue car."

Desi's heart jumped. "Did it have pink repair patches on it?" she asked.

She nodded. "That's it."

"What happened when Dora came out?"

The woman transferred the baby to her other hip. "Nothing really. She came out, talked a little with the other woman. They walked to the car, got in and drove off."

The witness's name was Ronit Shatkin. Desi took her contact information, thanked her and headed back to the Crown Vic.

Bryony Podeswa. How had she found out where Dorina was? And where had she taken her? She knocked on Flame's door. This time he answered.

"I thought you left by now," he said, crossing his arms.

"Was Dorina friends with Bryony Podeswa, Mistress Achlys?"

He twisted his lips. "I wouldn't call them friends, but they worked together at the mansion."

"Where would Bryony have taken her?"

He shrugged. "No idea. I steer clear of everyone at that place. I just do my work and get paid, that's it."

Desi walked back to the car and pulled out into the street. Her empty stomach was rumbling and a twinge in her temple told her a headache as forthcoming if she didn't eat soon. She was now in her twelfth working hour of the day, and she wasn't done yet. She patted her jacket pocket for a granola bar. It was empty. An idea of how to find Dorina glimmered in her mind. She had to get back to the station.

17

"We need to cut Podeswa loose," Desi said, breathless from galloping up the stairs.

Fin looked at her standing next to his desk, her chest heaving. "What?"

"You know what's going to happen when that lawyer Specchio gets here."

He crossed his arms. "Tell me, what's going to happen?"

"Same thing that happened with Biesu. A non-interview. Possession of a branding iron isn't illegal. It wasn't even hidden. We only have circumstantial evidence that Podeswa used it on Parker. Forensic might not find anything indicating it was used on Parker at all. They probably clean the thing after use."

"What're you saying?" Fin said.

"We kick Podeswa and tail her."

Fin looked doubtful. "Which will get us exactly what?"

"Our missing witness. Dorina was living in the mansion. She was the last one to see Sterling Parker alive. She escaped from Biesu because she was afraid she'd disappear, as her sister did. She went to Parker for help because he was already helping her with her immigration status. Then he died."

"Wait, back up. Where are you getting all this?"

Desi took a deep breath and told him what she'd found out from Flame and the neighbor.

"All right, but we've got Podeswa in the tank with a murder weapon found in her house. We can ask her where she took Dorina. We don't need to do surveillance."

"She's not going to say anything, especially with Specchio sitting next to her. If Specchio gets here, we're going to have to show her our whole hand and we don't want to do that, yet."

"So we bluff."

"So we tail Podeswa and find our witness. We got her spooked right now. She'll lead us to something."

"Even if we find this Dorina, what are the chances that she'll call Specchio and clam up, too?" Fin said.

"She's afraid of Biesu and wants to find her sister. We can get the DA to offer her a deal—one of those visas for crime victims."

Fin shook his head, his face full of doubt. "I think it's the wrong way to go and a waste of manpower. We've still got a pile of DVDs from Biesu's toss that we need to go through. Sterling Parker's branding could be on one of them. If it is, we can get an arrest warrant. Case closed. End of story."

A pain stabbed her skull. As it subsided, the image of the person who had told Bryony Podeswa that Dorina was hiding with Flame clicked in her mind. She knew exactly who had called Bryony.

She had no more time to waste arguing with Finbar McNab. She had to pull rank.

"Duly noted." She iced him with her eyes. "But I don't think it's the end of story at all. Since I'm lead on the case, it's my call. I'm releasing Bryony before Specchio gets here. You want to take the first surveillance shift?"

"And you?"

Her head whirled. She was going to faint. She lurched and clutched the desk.

Fin sprang up. "You all right?"

"I just need to sit." Black spots swam in front of her eyes.

He lowered her into his chair. "When was the last time you ate?"

"Lunch."

"Wait here."

He returned with water and a stale cheese Danish from a plate that someone had left in the break room. She drank and chewed the pastry slowly as he watched.

"I ran out of granola bars," she said.

"Shit, Nimmo, you gotta eat more than granola bars and the occasional sandwich."

She finished the Danish and chugged down the water as Fin watched. She felt a spurt of energy and dusted off her palms. "You're still doing the first shift on Podeswa."

Desi had her foot on the first step of the staircase when she heard Lt. Butler's voice. "Desi, gotta minute?"

Fuck. She halted. "Not really, LT."

"You can make one."

Butler disappeared inside her office, which meant there was no excuse. Desi trudged after her. "What's up?"

"I got a request from downtown for more details about the homicide. How close are we to solving this?"

Desi noted her use of the first-person plural with some irony. "Is this because it was in the paper?"

"Probably. It's caught their interest."

"We talking Robbery Homicide?" Desi said.

Butler nodded. Desi sat in the chair in front of the desk. "We need to locate the witness who's missing. She's the linchpin."

"Who's the missing witness?"

"The woman from Moldova, Dorina," Desi said.

"The illegal?"

"I have a lead and I'm on it."

Desi was hesitant to spell out her full theory after Butler had previously reamed her out for straying from her jurisdiction. Nor was she about to say that her lead involved surveillance. Butler would likely quash that because of budget concerns, although now that RHD had taken an interest in the case, she might be more amenable to authorizing the overtime. Still, Desi didn't want to risk the LT saying no. If they did get the solve, the LT would be happy to pay out the overtime.

Plus, Desi strongly suspected that she could talk Fin into foregoing the full amount of OT that surveillance entailed, given his hunger to grab credit for clearing the case.

Butler eyed her with doubt. "You going to tell me what the lead is?"

Desi had to give her something to pass on to downtown. "I have a witness who saw Bryony Podeswa drive off with the missing woman from the place where she was hiding out. I think Podeswa took her somewhere."

Desi felt Butler's assessing gaze.

"Podeswa's the dominatrix?" the lieutenant asked.

Desi nodded. The lieutenant drew a deep breath. "I'm going to do everything I can to keep the case, but if we don't get this solved in short order, we're going to have to pass it on to RHD."

"I know, LT, I know."

After Desi disappeared downstairs to order Bryony Podeswa's release, Fin put on his jacket, ready to head out to the first surveillance shift.

His desk phone rang. He answered. It was David Parker, Sterling Parker's father. "We just wanted to check on the progress of the investigation," he said. "There was something about it on the Times website."

"We've made a lot of progress, Mr. Parker, but no arrests yet. We think we've found the weapon, though."

"That's something. We're still wondering how this happened."

"We're figuring it out. When we have definitive answers, you'll be the first to know."

Parker thanked him and rang off.

Fin walked over to the sign-out board and as he was about to note his destination, a growing sense of bitterness and resentment gnawed at him. Desi was endangering the whole investigation due to this harebrained idea of cutting Podeswa loose. She'd be in the wind in five minutes. There were other angles to pursue. And now the victim's parents were pressing for an arrest.

He glanced over his shoulder. Butler was shuffling papers on her desk. He didn't want to do this, but he had to. He owed it to Joy and David Parker. Police served the victims of crime not each other. He set down the marker and strode over to Butler's door and rapped with his knuckles.

"Got a minute, LT?"

Desi barreled through No Holds Barred into the rear patio. With some luck, the happy hour would still be going on and he would still be there.

It was dark on the patio and with the sparse light from the fairy lights, it was difficult to make out who sat at the tables. Far from the happy hour being almost over, the place was humming.

She headed toward the table where she'd found him the last time. As she approached, a reedy figure stood and walked behind the table along the fence in the opposite direction. She dashed ahead and intercepted him before he reached the barrier of the second table.

"Mr. Niedermeier, I need a word," she said quietly.

His face crumpled. "What now?"

"I just have a couple questions. Should we go over here?" She signaled a corner of the patio that was occupied only by shadows.

He pursed his lips. "Do I have an option?"

"Not unless you want to come down to the police station."

He moved to the corner.

"Are you acquainted with Bryony Podeswa, aka Mistress Achlys?"

"Yeah," he said in a resigned tone.

"You worked with or for her at Thanatos?"

"I was an extra in a couple of movies she worked on."

"You've kept in touch?"

"Not really."

"But you called her the other day to let her know Dorina was here."

He rubbed his chin. "So?"

"Why did you do that?"

"She was going to get Flame in trouble with Biesu. He already told Flame to stay away from her. Flame just felt sorry for her."

"Bryony came and picked her up. Where did she take her?"

He hiked his shoulders. "Back to Biesu's mansion, I guess."

Desi studied him. He seemed to be telling the truth.

"Any idea where else she could've taken her?"

"How the hell should I know? I really didn't care where the fuck the bitch went as long as she was away from Flame."

Desi paused. What else did she need? Niedermeier pivoted to step away.

"One more thing," she said.

He turned, an annoyed look on his face.

"Did you happen to hear any of what Dorina said to Flame?"

"I don't eavesdrop," he spat before turning his back to her.

That was the only thing in their conversation that Desi felt was a lie.

Desi edged forward in the snaking line of cars at the Inn-N-Out drive-thru. The Danish had disappeared quickly from her stomach and before she started the drive back to West LA, she realized she'd better eat something more substantial. She didn't want to faint again.

Jason Niedermeier knew he was turning Dorina over to people who would hurt her. Jealousy was a powerful motivator.

Bryony had to be working for Biesu. With a bit of luck, she would lead them right to where they had stashed Dorina.

Biesu wanted whatever Dorina had on him that linked him to her sister's disappearance. She'd probably be safe until she gave that up.

Her phone rang. She glanced at the caller ID. Shit. Now what? She picked up.

"Desi, where are you?" Lt. Butler sounded testy. A feeling bit Desi's gut. This was not going to be good.

She mustered up a light tone. "I'm on my way into the station, LT," she said.

"That's not what I asked. I repeat, where are you?"

"In the Valley."

"All right, I don't really know what you're doing there and neither does your partner, but I want to go home, and since it's going to be a while until you get back here, I'm going to tell you over the phone. I'm making McNab the lead on the Sterling Parker homicide investigation, effective immediately."

Desi's stomach crunched into a ball.

Butler continued. "I know McNab can be a pain in the ass, and you're a good detective, but he's got a lot more experience on homicides. I'm putting him in charge." She softened her tone. "I realize it's not the same since Sam died."

Desi found her voice. "You think I can't handle an investigation without Sam?"

"It's not that at all. You're not taking care of yourself. Let's talk tomorrow about getting you some time off. For now, I've told McNab to go get that suspect that you just released. I don't have the budget for surveillance. You should have cleared that with me. You deliberately withheld that."

Time off? Desi's head spun. "But ..." She realized it was useless to protest. "Roger that, Lieutenant." She hung up. McNab. That motherfucking weasel. He'd done it again and now he'd won.

Fin pulled into the driveway leading to Bryony Podeswa's converted garage behind her Corolla and got out. He signaled to Len Martinez to monitor the rear of the building while he did the door-knocking.

Martinez nodded and rounded the corner of the cottage. The LT had assigned him to accompany Fin to bring back Bryony to the station since Desi was god-knows-where pursuing her own little tangents. His chat with Butler had taken longer than he expected. By the time he got downstairs, Bryony was long gone from the station.

Fin strode to the door and pounded it with the side of his fist. "Ms. Podeswa, police." No answer. He hammered again.

A screen door slapped behind him. He wheeled, hand on the butt of his weapon in his hip holster.

A middle-aged man in a wife-beater and beltless jeans that exposed the elastic waistband on his boxers stood on the back step.

"She's not home. I saw her go out," he said.

Fin flashed his badge. "LAPD. Any idea when she'll be back?"

He shrugged. "She comes and goes, but she had a suitcase with her, so maybe she went on a trip."

Shit. "That's her car, isn't it?" Fin pointed to the beater.

"Yeah, that's hers, but I saw her waiting out front for somebody."

"You see what kind of car picked her up?"

"Sorry. The kid started crying, and I didn't see."

Martinez joined him.

"We're too late. She's in the wind," Fin said. "Fuck!" He pounded the side of the garage with the heel of his fist.

Martinez addressed the neighbor. "Any idea where she might've gone? Has she ever mentioned family or anything?"

"Nah, she really isn't very friendly, kinda weird, you know? Keeps to herself, works off hours."

Fin handed him a business card. "Can you give us a call when she comes back?"

He nodded.

Fin walked with Martinez back to the car, shaking his head. "I knew it, I fucking knew it. Cutting her loose was a massive mistake."

Martinez got in, shifting his bulk over the wheel. The guy was so big he practically filled the car. "Listen, we all make bad calls. Desi's a solid detective, and she's been through some shit in this department."

"Haven't we all?" Fin said. Martinez looked at Fin curiously. Fin had to change the subject, fast. "What happened to Desi?"

Martinez's focus remained on the street. "Better you ask her, bro. That's all I'm gonna say."

Fin had Martinez drop him off at his SUV in the station's parking lot so he could get a Red Bull he had left in it. He was going to need it to stay awake to watch at least a couple of Biesu's recorded S&M sessions. There was a pile to get through.

Fin beeped open the SUV, retrieved the Red Bull, cracked it open and took a slurp. He really hadn't wanted to complain—again. He knew he was trying Butler's patience, and nobody liked snitches but goddamn, Desi had left him with little choice. And ultimately, he was proven right—Podeswa had skipped out.

He texted Butler that they'd missed Podeswa, pocketed the phone and started walking to the station door. Headlights bounced into the parking lot entrance. A car pulled up beside him and as the window rolled down, the beam cast by a light pole caught the driver's face. Desi. Of course. Well, he had to get the confrontation over and done with.

"Listen," he said. "I know you're pissed off, but just so you know, Podeswa's in the wind. A neighbor saw her leave with a suitcase."

"If you'd tailed her from the station, we'd know where she went, wouldn't we? But you were too busy jerking off Butler. What can I say? You're the murder cop with all the experience, after all." Her voice dripped with sarcasm.

"Butler just wants to solve the case. It's nothing against you, Desi, really."

"Butler wants to clear the case so it can up the bad numbers on this month's Compstat report, and you want credit for the solve. Where the fuck does that leave me, McNab?"

Fin felt too weary to argue. "Listen, I'm gonna start reviewing those CCTV DVDs from the Biesu toss. You can help or not."

She rolled up the window and gunned the gas. He leapt out of the way. The wheel of her car missed his foot by ten inches.

As Desi tramped up the stairs to the squad room, the rage that had overcome her when she saw Fin in the parking lot melted with each step. She was too tired to carry that burden, but a weight of dejection landed on her shoulders in its place. She needed to go home and surf. Maybe the lieutenant was right.

She should just say to hell with it, abandon the case, take some time off. Maybe she really couldn't work a complex case without Sam. She seemed to take nothing but missteps.

Maybe she should even think about doing something else, something with less stress. Like teaching surfing. There couldn't be a lot of politics involved in that.

As she neared the top of the stairs, she heard a rumble of voices in the squad room. Len Martinez was usually working alone at this hour. Somebody else must be working a case hard. She turned the corner of the landing and was hit with the sight of boxy shoulders mantling a wide back.

She stopped. It couldn't be.

"Hey, Desi," Len sang out. "What're you doing here this late?"

The back twisted. It was. It was him. What the fuck was he doing here?

"You know Rondell Nichols from Hollywood, right?" Len's voice sounded hollow as if he was calling down a tunnel.

Rondell beamed at her, exposing a row of teeth white as corn kernels. "Desi, it's been a while."

Steps shuffled behind her. She turned.

Fin entered the squad room. She gathered herself. "Yep, it has." She addressed Len. "I'm just signing in the Vic then I'm outta here." She turned to the logbook and scrawled her name and time. Behind her, she heard Len introduce Fin and Rondell.

"What brings you to West LA?" Fin asked.

Desi flipped through the logbook, pretending to hunt for something as she listened. "I just finished a witness interview a couple blocks from here, so I thought I'd stop in, see who was around. Turns out you guys work later than I thought."

"We're working a homicide," Fin said.

"Looks like my instincts were right on, then. We have an opening coming up on our squad, and it looks like we're going to get the green light to fill it."

"Good to know," Fin said.

"I wanted to spread the word. We'd like to get a detective with experience, not a greenhorn," Rondell said.

Desi went to her desk and grabbed her pen and pad for something to do as she feigned disinterest in her conversation. Sterling Parker's DVD boxes on Fin's desk caught her eye. He'd never returned them to the evidence room. She should report him to Butler in the morning. Tit for tat.

Her cell phone beeped with a text.

Up for a beer? I'm in Venice.

Denny Comiskey. She couldn't handle him right now on top of everything else. She texted him back.

Bad time, but I'll take a rain check.

She suddenly felt crowded. She needed to get away from the station, be alone. She strode past the huddle of men.

"Catch ya on the flipside, guys."

"Later," Len said.

"I should go, too. I'll walk you out, Desi," Rondell said.

She jogged down the staircase.

He caught up with her in a couple large strides in the parking lot. She rounded on him as she felt his presence bearing down on her.

"What the fuck do you want, Rondell? Three years I hear nothing from you, and now you're bugging the shit out of me? I don't want anything to do with you."

"I want you to apply for the Hollywood job I was talking about."

"Are you fucking kidding me?"

"We have a new lieutenant, so you'll be coming in clean, and I won't be there. I'm heading downtown to the cold case squad. I can put in a good word for you, and it'll carry some weight."

"And I'm supposed to forget how you fucked me over just like that?"

She snapped her fingers.

"Better late than never."

"That's your excuse?"

"I fucked up. I should've admitted our affair to my wife and to the LT, I know that now. I got scared of losing everything, and somehow it seemed the easiest thing to lose was you. But I want to make it up to you. Think about your career. You're a damn good detective, Desi. Take my offer."

"Think about my career? That's rich coming from you. Your sexual harassment charge against me almost tanked my whole career. I was lucky the union worked out a deal so I could land here. Why the fuck should I ever trust you when you stabbed me right to the backbone? After everything you said to me when we were together? Fuck you, Mr. Hollywood Detective of the Year. Fuck. You!" she screamed the last word and bolted to her car.

As she screeched out of the parking lot, she caught Fin standing between the rows of cars, staring at her. Shit.

Only one of Fin's housemates was home. Jesus was prone on the couch stuffing sour-cream flavored potato chips into his mouth as he watched a shoot-'em-up on TV. He was surrounded by a semi-circle of crumbs littering both the floor and the couch.

"Do you actually ever get any chips into your mouth?" Fin said in annoyance.

"Huh?" Jesus halted his mouth mid-crunch and looked at him disinterestedly.

"Forget it. Where's Ron?"

"Went out with some chick he met online. Third date so he's hoping he won't be home tonight. He's going to ask her if she's got any friends."

"Great," Fin muttered as he proceeded upstairs.

Ginger's watchful eyes were waiting for him in the bedroom. When she had left, she'd taken all the presents he'd ever given her. But not the portrait. Out of everything, that perhaps had hurt the most. He'd put his heart into that painting. It had taken months to finish, and he considered it his best work to date. But she didn't want it, like she didn't want him.

The worst part was that her rejection had soured him completely on art, the one thing that gave him joy, besides, of course, Ginger. He hadn't even been able to pick up a pencil and pad to sketch.

He'd taken to drawing more since Ginger had complained about the strong smell of oil paint. He'd packed up his palette and brushes in a box and put it in the garage, like a set of bald tires. Then all the shit had happened at work, Ginger had left, and now he couldn't draw or paint.

Ginger's brown eyes stared at him from the canvas, harsh with accusation. Yes, he'd gotten what he wanted, the lead on the investigation, but somehow it didn't seem like a triumph. It felt ... dirty. Shameful. He walked over and turned the portrait to face the wall.

Fin undressed and got into bed with his laptop. He inserted one of the CCTV CDs into the computer and pressed play. He had decided to watch at home in comfort instead of at the station. A scene of a dominatrix thrashing a tied up, blindfolded man with a riding crop sprang onto the screen. He pressed fast forward. No need to watch in real time.

His mind wandered to the scene he had witnessed between Desi and Rondell Nichols. So that was Desi's story. Nichols had treated her like shit. No wonder she was embittered. And now there was an opening in the Hollywood Division. Desi was unlikely to go for it, which left the path wide open.

18

Now in her wetsuit, Desi trotted along Venice Beach to the obsidian sea. The moon hung like a hook in the tarred sky. Except for a few dogwalkers, skateboarders, and the jagged silhouettes of homeless bodies lying under palm trees on the grassy strip, the beach and boardwalk were empty.

Night was the time when Desi liked surfing the most, when she could claim the ocean to herself. She waded into the waves, feeling the wind bite her face and blow through her hair. She breathed the briny air deep into her lungs as she pushed her legs against the incoming tide until she got deep enough to hop onto the board and paddle. Her arm muscles felt the strain that came after a period of disuse.

The ache felt good, a sign that she was accomplishing something. When she'd paddled far enough, she turned the board and sat astraddle for a moment, looking at the shoreline, polka-dotted with amber and white lights.

The night was clear. To the north, the Ferris wheel on the Santa Monica pier flashed gaudy neon stripes. To the south, the illuminated stacks of the electric power plant at Redondo Beach poked the sky.

She twisted her head behind her. On the horizon sat the cigar shapes of oil tankers. An oil rig twinkled. A swell was building. She concentrated on the growing wave as it rushed toward her, gathering force with momentum, then she started paddling to get up to speed to hit that crucial moment to leap to a crouch on the board and stay on it, knees knifed, as the wave crested.

Now it was a balancing act, feeling the movement of the water unfurling beneath the board and intuitively shifting weight and limbs to tame it.

The wave diminished to a dribble of foam. Desi hopped off the board, feeling more alive, lighter and cleaner, than she had in days.

She turned around and did it again for three more waves until she hauled herself and the board out of the water, heavy with physical exhaustion that outweighed the mental confusion. Now she'd be able to sleep.

She trudged back home, peeled off her wetsuit and jumped in the shower, letting the waterfall of hot water cascade over her head and back until the glass shower stall was steamed in. She lathered herself over and over until her skin squeaked. McNab, Rondell, Butler, Denny, all of them washed off her and swirled down the drain.

The next day, Lieutenant Butler caught Desi in the break room as she was pouring a cup of coffee.

"Desi, I got a special for you. The captain just got an email from Council Member Hounanian's office, which he passed on to me, which I just forwarded to you. Report back to me by end of watch, so I can tell the captain we took action. And before you start whining, I got no one else to send."

The Blood Room

Fuck. When the Westside council member called the captain, it always meant some bullshit complaint from his constituents: graffiti, people living in RVs parked at the curb, loud parties.

She sighed as she sat down at her desk and called up her inbox. She skimmed through the forwarded email and rolled her eyes. This one was bullshittier than usual.

Drawing a deep breath, she considered complaining to the LT anyway. She was major crimes detective, for crissake. Patrol should be handling this.

Butler was clearly giving her busy work to keep her off the homicide.

But then she reconsidered. Not worth it. She'd do it, score some brownie points. She picked up her coffee cup and notebook.

She passed Fin in the parking lot.

"Hey, where are you off to so bright and early?" he called.

"Going to see a man about a dog," Desi said without stopping.

Desi looked around the living room at the expectant faces of eight older residents of the upscale Brentwood neighborhood who had complained to the councilman that their cats and dogs had been disappearing.

An elderly lady, a cloud of snowy hair framing a birdlike face, gave her a friendly smile, which she returned.

"Have a seat, Detective." Sam Cohen, the host and group organizer, gestured toward the dining chair pulled around the coffee table for extra seating. "Can I get you coffee?"

"No thanks. I can't stay long. I have witnesses to interview on another case."

A pre-emptive lie. Desi sat in the indicated chair.

The elderly woman nudged a plate of oatmeal raisin cookies toward Desi, who smiled noncommittally.

"So, I understand your pets have gone missing," she prompted, flipping open her notebook. She still couldn't quite believe she was investigating this.

Sam unfolded a square of paper on top of the ziggurat of landscape photography books in the middle of the table. "This is what's been going on."

It was a map of the neighborhood marked with eight numbers and a corresponding key listing the pets and dates they were last seen.

"Jim." Sam pointed to a bearded man on the couch who looked familiar. He obediently raised his hand, "and I canvassed the area to see how many pets had gone missing. As you can see, the disappearances started four months ago. All expensive breeds."

Jim leaned forward, elbows on his knees. "There's a pattern that makes me think there's something deliberate about it. It started with cats, then small dogs, then bigger dogs. It's not random."

Desi studied the list to verify what Jim was saying, wondering if he was Jim Hendrie, the noted movie director. She cast her eyes around the circle.

"Has anyone noticed any strangers hanging around the neighborhood? Any odd bowls of food or water?"

"There's a shabby Econoline van that parks on my street at night," the elderly lady said.

"That 'shabby' van belongs to my son," said a man, whose too-perfect hairline belied the presence of implants.

"What time of day did the animals disappear?" Desi asked.

"Mostly night," Sam said. Heads nodded.

"I let my dog out at night in the back yard to do his business, and he never came back," said a woman pushing large, black-rimmed glasses up her nose. "Mine's the Pekinese."

"No unusual barking?" Heads shook.

"We're completely baffled as to why our neighborhood would be targeted," Sam said. "It's really quite worrying. What will they try next: home invasions? We have a lot of elderly residents."

Desi closed her notepad. "There's been a cat and dog shortage since the pandemic. People emptied shelters for pets to keep them company at home, so animals are getting high prices right now.

I'd say that's the motive. And once their scheme worked the first time, the thieves came back, getting better and bolder with each theft.

"They probably chose this neighborhood for the simple reason that it offers easy access to Sunset Boulevard and the freeway, and it's all single-family homes with open yards. I suggest checking Craigslist to see if any of your pets are being sold online. If you find any you think are yours, call me."

Desi took out a wad of business cards from her pocket and handed it to Sam, who took one and passed it on.

"I'll request patrol to step up neighborhood checks at night. Keep your pets inside or on a leash. Don't let them roam by themselves, even in your yard. Somebody could be luring the animals with food that contains tranquilizers. Makes sure you have good photos of them, too, for identification purposes."

"That's it?" said the old lady. "No fingerprinting?"

"Nothing to fingerprint, ma'am," Desi said. "Even though we'll have extra patrols, the best leads will come from residents. Stay alert. If you notice anything unusual, call me."

Sam accompanied her to the front door. "Thank you so much for coming, Detective. I know you must have bigger crimes to handle, but for some people, their animals are all they've got."

"I understand." Desi's eyes fixed on a burgundy tufted velvet couch sitting outside the garage.

"My son doesn't want it after I went to all the trouble of dragging it outside and throwing my back out in the process, so it's going to stay there for a while. Kids." Sam shook his head.

Desi smiled. "Get back to me if you find anything about the pets."

Back at the station, she wrote up the report for Butler and delved into a couple of stale robberies and a gang shooting, making notes of leads to follow up. Due to the Parker case, she was behind on everything else.

She powered through the evening to catch up on files and phone calls, deliberately avoiding McNab, answering him on monosyllables if he addressed her. What did he expect? A hug and a kiss?

She translated her anger and frustration to focusing on the backlog of files.

When she heard Len Martinez call out good night to her, she sat back. What time was it? After eleven. She should go home. She'd done more than enough for a day. She powered down the computer, stood, gathered her purse and headed out. On the way, she couldn't resist passing McNab's desk, which she'd carefully avoided all day.

Sterling Parker's DVDs were still there. She halted. Something had bothered her all along about those DVDs. Then she felt a click in her brain. She went to the break room, brewed a pot of strong coffee, poured herself a mug, and settled at her desk with the DVDs.

The guy at the porn store in Chatsworth had said the Overexposed movies were hardcore and were now off the market. So where had Sterling Parker obtained them? Possibly directly from Biesu or Thanatos. But they hadn't found any other copies of these DVDs during the search. Biesu didn't seem to have a stock of them.

She slid the first DVD into her computer's DVD tray, "Dungeon of Hades." The Roman numerals on the box gave its production date as three years ago. The movie opened with a dominatrix whipping a naked man wearing a hood and a dog collar while he crawled on all fours.

"Jesus Christ," she muttered.

She fast-forwarded, slowing to study every new scene and actor. The production quality was low. Shadows leered from the walls. The audio sounded tinny. There was no sequential plot linking the scenes.

Then she realized what she was watching — scenes of actual BDSM sessions. This was what the hidden cameras were for. The subjects' faces were disguised by hoods and blindfolds, but did these people really know they were being taped?

She paused the video to take a closer look at the domme's chest. It was marked by a long scar. She'd seen some of that scar before, on Bryony Podeswa.

Desi finished the first DVD, then slid in "Midnight Soul," also dated from three years ago. This one featured Flame as the torturer, who was immediately recognizable by his trademark tattoos. Bryony was his accomplice in several scenes.

She sped through the DVD. The scenes were hard to watch. Until she caught a long metal instrument in Bryony's hand. She paused the video. It was the brand, the crossed oval at one end burning with a red glow.

The camera followed the brand as it moved toward its target and met it, searing a section of anonymous flesh. A scream curdled her stomach. Flame had lied about never witnessing branding.

After jotting down the time of the branding scene, Desi fast-forwarded the video until the end.

Maybe this was where Sterling Parker had gotten the idea of being branded.

She inserted the DVD titled "The Blood Room" and pressed play. A black hood appeared, the head lolling slightly. The camera pulled back to reveal that the head belonged to a naked woman, spread-eagled on an X-shaped rack, bound with leather straps at the wrists and ankles. Desi halted the tape and studied her. Young, slight build.

She released the pause. A naked man wearing a black hood approached her with a cat-o-nine-tails. He hit her several times. She stirred but her head lolled. She seemed drugged. "I want to see your pain!" he yelled at her. "Scream!"

The woman picked up her head, as if trying to comply but could utter no more than grunts, and her head fell to the side. He flailed the whip against her over and over, but she seemed to be unconscious.

He flung the whip aside, placed his hands around her neck and squeezed. She gasped and struggled against him. He let go suddenly and whipped off her hood. She gulped air in ragged breaths.

Then the man moved in on her neck again. The camera zoomed in on her face and the bracelet of hands choking her windpipe.

He had taken off her hood to watch her die.

Her gut churning, Desi paused the video and scrutinized the woman's face. Pointy chin, fine blond hair, watery blue irises that peered out of heavy black-mascara nests. It looked familiar. She took out her cell phone and compared the woman's face to the picture on her phone from Flavia.

It resembled Dorina, but it wasn't her. Then she knew.

She found the photo of the two girls she had taken from Dorina's room at Biesu's mansion and held it side-by-side to the woman on screen. It was her sister. Desi was willing to bet her name was Ruslana Ludmila Cojocaru.

She released the pause. The man shook the woman by the neck like a ragdoll. Her eyes bulged, she struggled uselessly then finally she appeared to give up. Her body went limp under his hands and her eyes vacated into the non-seeing stare of death.

The camera jostled and screen cut to black. Desi fast-forwarded but the tape had ended.

A tremor rippled through her body. She laid her head down on the desk, and closed her eyes, taking deep breaths to steady her jitters. It took over a minute but then a tremulous calm overcame her.

This was the evidence Dorina had found, incontrovertible evidence that her sister was murdered, evidence that could get Dorina killed, too. Desi could only hope that it hadn't already.

Desi refilled her coffee mug and returned to her desk. She punched up a database and filled in search terms for unidentified bodies: white female, age fifteen to forty, from three years ago to the present. She'd try Los Angeles County first.

She scrolled through numerous entries and photos. Most were women found lifeless on urban streets. A couple looked like Dorina's sister, but the eye color was wrong, or they had needle tracks or tattoos in places that Desi knew from the tape that her vic did not have.

Several Jane Does had turned up in wooded areas and the desert. Those were more likely body dumps, so she scrutinized the photos, any identifying marks listed—tattoos, scars, birthmarks, moles—and the causes of death, looking for asphyxiation/strangulation, and contusions on the neck, wrists, and ankles.

She exhausted the list with no match, so she widened the parameters of the search to surrounding counties. Outside LA, the number of entries decreased dramatically.

She scrolled on, sipping coffee. Then an entry caught her eye.

The body of a young female had been found out in San Bernardino County. Her heart sped. She stared at the photo of the woman's wax-like death mask, then compared it to the childhood photo with Dorina.

It was the sister. She was positive.

According to the statement of facts, a beekeeper searching for a remote spot to put his hives had come across a hand partially protruding from the sand.

Investigators found the body buried in a shallow grave at the end of a dry creek bed in a canyon.

The coroner put the time of death as approximately six to eight months prior.

Dante Smith of the San Bernardino County Sheriff's Department was listed as the investigating detective.

Desi called Smith's phone number, not expecting an answer at three-fourteen in the morning, and left a voicemail.

She returned to viewing the video, scouring the background for any tell that could help narrow down its location. The room had bare cement block walls. Biesu's dungeon was fancier, more polished.

It was another place with an X-rack. It looked like a garage or some type of industrial warehouse. A storage unit, maybe?

The sharp ring of her phone smashed the silence. Her heart leapt and crashed. She answered.

"Dante Smith, SBSD, you called?"

"I did but I wasn't expecting you to call back at this hour."

"I have my desk phone forwarded to my cell phone and I keep my cell phone by my bed."

He couldn't be married. "I appreciate it since I'm not getting any sleep tonight. I think I got an ID on a Jane Doe of yours."

"I'm trying to recall the one you're looking at. Is that the one the beekeeper found?"

"That's the one."

She heard a rustle of bed covers and then Smith seemed more awake. "Yeah, I remember it. The trail on that one was as cold as they come and never got any warmer. She never matched any reported missing persons," he said. "Strangled, right?"

"Yep."

"There was a weird aspect to that one. The body had been cleaned with hydrogen peroxide. We couldn't get any forensics on her. Nothing."

"They knew to eliminate any traces. Not your garden variety killers then," Desi said.

"Agreed. It suggests some sophistication. We had a couple departments look at her as a possible serial killer victim, but that hydrogen peroxide made her an outlier. She didn't fit any MOs. Who's your vic?"

"I think she was trafficked from Eastern Europe and got into a hardcore BDSM scene. I found a possible sister but she's in the wind."

"You got any ID on the dead woman?"

"Possibly Ruslana Ludmila Cojocaru. I've got an old photo of her I can send over. If I find the younger sister, you might be able to close this one yet."

"Appreciate it. Hey, come to think of it, one of your guys was asking about her a while ago, too."

"You remember who?"

He paused. "It was a weird name, can't recall it off the top of my head."

Desi knew who it had to be, the same cop who'd been poking around about illegals. "Hargitay? Al Hargitay?"

"That's it. That's exactly who it was."

Desi thanked him and hung up. Why had Hargitay been interested in a Jane Doe out in San Bernardino? Although he could've checked her out for any missing person's case. Detectives often checked out John and Jane Does as a matter of course.

She should call McNab, as much as she didn't want to. He'd find some way to grab the credit for her legwork. But if she didn't call him, he'd get pissed off, go running to Butler and she'd be in even more trouble. Plus, it would be a dig to wake him up and let him know that she'd been working while he'd been sleeping. She picked up the phone.

He answered with a sleep-coated growl. "This better be good."

"I found the missing sister, a Jane Doe dumped out in San Berdoo. She was killed during rough sex that was caught on tape."

"What?" He sounded awake now.

"Remember Sterling Parker's DVDs? One of them has her murder recorded on it. I think Dorina found the DVD in Biesu's house and gave it to Sterling Parker for safekeeping. Maybe he didn't know it was her sister, maybe he did. Biesu discovered the missing disc and Dorina ran. She called Parker for help that night."

"I'll be right in."

She hung up, got herself a fresh coffee and started watching the third DVD. It also looked to be taped in a room made of concrete block.

An odd shadow moved across the bottom of the wall, pointed like the tip of something, as a dominatrix rode a man on all fours, yanking a studded dog's collar tight around the man's neck, making his head jerk back. The camera zoomed in on the collar and the hand gripping it. The hand.

Desi rewound the tape, paused it and examined the fingernails. She knew where Dorina had to be.

19

Desi and Fin sat in the Crown Vic in the feathery darkness down the street from Al Hargitay's house, formulating their plan for door-knocking the detective.

"You sure about this? It's four-thirty in the goddamn morning," Fin said. "If we're wrong, he's going to be pissed. He'll complain to the LT."

"I told you, I saw Hargitay's wife's fingernails. They were full of clay, just like they were when I went there the other day. She's into making all these ceramic pots and stuff. Their whole house is full of them.

"And it fits. He and his wife could be into this whole BDSM scene. I'm willing to bet Biesu is paying Hargitay to quash any complaint about on-set injuries. He would've known to wash Jane Doe's body with hydrogen peroxide and then he went out to San Bernardino to check out if they'd got any forensics or anything else on her.

"I'm sure that job alone got him either the boat or the Tesla. When I asked him, he said he'd made good investments. He totally tried to shove me off the trail, too." Desi suddenly straightened. Her gaze trained on the house. "Attention: K-Mart shoppers. We got action." She pointed to the garage.

A light had flicked on. Two seconds later, the door rolled up with a loud hum, exposing the boat and the Tesla next to it. The car's brake lights glowed then it started reversing out of the garage.

"Scoot down in the seat so he doesn't see us," Desi said, sliding down in her seat. Fin did the same.

A woman scurried out of the garage. Deb Hargitay. The car stopped at the end of the driveway.

Desi rolled down her window to see if she could catch any of the conversation. A jumble of syllables floated on the clear morning air. She strained to hear. By the tone, they seemed to be arguing.

Deb's tone suddenly rose an octave. "She's his problem, not ours! Just dump her on his doorstep, Al! For crissake, grow a pair." She thumped the roof of the car with her hand.

"I think Dorina's in that car. We have to intercept him," Desi said.

"We should call for backup." Fin fished for his phone.

"No time." The car was already reversing down the drive. "As soon as he's off his property and in the public right-of-way, cut him off. No lights so he'll be surprised. I'll get out and talk to him. Seeing me will unnerve him. I'll make up some bullshit about the case. You take the passenger side. Get Dorina if she's in the back seat. He might have put her in the trunk."

Fin's lips twitched. He nodded tightly and gripped the steering wheel with both hands. Hargitay was reversing into a curve in the street now, halting to change gears into drive. He started to pull forward. Fin rubbed one palm on his thighs, then the other.

"You okay?" Desi said.

"Yep."

Desi straightened. "Here we go. Get ready."

Fin turned the ignition key and shifted the Crown Vic into drive. Hargitay was accelerating down the street. Fin's fists clenched and unclenched the steering wheel.

"Go!" Desi said. "Block him!"

Fin clutched the steering wheel, staring straight ahead. Desi shot him a look of incredulity.

"What the fuck, McNab! Go! Come on! He's getting away!"

Fin didn't seem to hear her. He didn't move. He was frozen.

Ahead, the embers of Hargitay's taillights rounded the corner and were extinguished by the night.

"For fuck's sake!" Desi bounded out of the passenger door and ran around to the driver's door. It was locked. She pounded on the window with the heel of her fist. "Open up!"

She threw up her hands, letting them drop against her sides with a slap. She closed her eyes for a second to calm down. She walked slowly back to the car and slid into the passenger's seat, a bell clanging somewhere in her mind.

Fin was as still as a marble sculpture. The detectives' association newsletter. She now knew who Fin was, why he'd transferred to West LA.

"You were the detective who killed the kid during a pursuit, weren't you?"

Fin swiveled his head at her. His vacant look gave her the answer.

Desi called in Hargitay's car then forced Fin to get in the passenger's seat. She rocketed down the freeway, weaving in and out of lanes to avoid the thickening morning traffic. Biesu's mansion seemed the logical place that Hargitay would take Dorina. The place had already been searched. Biesu would think he was in the clear.

As she sped along, the call came in. Al Hargitay had been pulled over. No one else was in the vehicle.

"Goddammit!" She thumped the steering wheel with the heel of her hand.

She braked and slalomed across lanes to the next exit where she knew there was an all-night diner. She glanced at Fin. He was practically catatonic. She couldn't believe he'd risked the whole investigation like that.

As she settled into a booth and ordered coffee, Fin went to wash his face. He seemed to be finally coming out of his stricken state. She took advantage of his absence to search on her phone for the stories about Fin's "accident."

An article in the Times popped right up.

> Cop Runs Over, Kills Girl
>
> By Chloe Quinn
>
> An off-duty detective ran over and killed an eight-year-old girl last night as he pursued a suspect through a residential neighborhood of South Los Angeles.
>
> 'This is a devastating incident,' police Chief Aida Ballesteros said at a press conference. 'I think I speak for all members of the department when I say that our prayers are with this family at this time.'
>
> The detective involved, a 15-year LAPD veteran, has not been identified as per department policy. He has been suspended pending the results of an internal investigation, Ballesteros said.
>
> The accident occurred shortly after 10 p.m. when the detective, who had just ended his shift, was driving home, police said. He spotted a suspect wanted in a gang-related homicide who was believed to have fled to Mexico.
>
> The fugitive was driving a pickup truck in the opposite direction. The detective did a u-turn and pursued the suspect, who turned into a residential neighborhood.
>
> The victim, Genesis Zendaya, ran out from between two parked cars into the street to retrieve a ball, and was struck by the detective's car.
>
> Her uncle Pedro Zendaya, who was visibly distraught, said the officer should have turned on his siren or flashing lights as a warning. 'Why was he conducting a high-speed chase through this neighborhood? Kids are playing all over the place here,' he said.

Victoria Castillo, a local activist, said the case underscores a lack of respect by police for communities of color. 'Authorities place a lower value on human life in our neighborhoods,' she said.

Jesus.

Desi had told him to keep the headlights off. It was dark, a residential street. He had to speed up and overtake a vehicle. All the same elements as that night.

No wonder he'd had some type of panic attack. Shit. A vague sense of guilt stole over her. But she hadn't known.

Desi scrolled through a subsequent article about a candlelight prayer vigil held for the little girl, and then a damning exclusive from the same reporter quoting anonymous sources saying the detective had turned off his headlights when he turned into the residential streets so the fugitive would think he'd lost his pursuer. He also failed to call for pursuit backup.

A host of comments followed the stories, some lambasting the police department while some blamed the victim's parents for letting their children play outside late at night and not teaching them about running into the road.

What a shitstorm. Desi remembered it had ignited debate within police ranks, as well. She pocketed the phone as she spotted Fin heading toward the booth.

The waitress slid two coffees to go across the table. Wisps of steam curled from the cup opening and vanished in the air as Fin slipped into the bench seat, avoiding Desi's eyes. He wrapped both his hands around the paper cup, looking into it. He took a sip and looked up to meet her gaze. Without his swagger, he seemed almost like another man.

"I'm sorry," he said.

"I wish you'd told me. I would've never let you drive."

He twirled the cup between his hands and nodded. "It's the first time that's happened, for the record."

"Weren't you cleared by BSU to come back to work?"

He sighed. "Yeah, but sitting in a shrink's office is a lot different than being on the job. I thought I could handle it. But I guess I couldn't." He stared out of the window into the parking lot illuminated by a flashing neon sign "Open 24 Hours" that threw alternating waves of pink and purple light over the parked cars. "You gonna tell the LT?"

Desi stared at Fin. "You know I have to tell the LT."

"It'll mean my job."

"I don't have a choice. Freezing up could put an officer's life on the line."

He looked at her. "One thing I learned from that whole mess, you always have a choice."

She wanted to find sympathy for him, but he was sure making it hard. "Yeah, like you had a choice to rat me out to Butler."

He gulped coffee. "You're right. I deserve whatever I have coming."

"Let's go. I'm taking you back to the station."

"If Hargitay doesn't have Dorina, where else could she be?"

Desi eyed him. Did he really think she was going to let him continue on the case when he had just fucked it up?

"I'm taking you back to the station," she repeated. "The LT will be in soon."

Back on the freeway, they zoomed in acute silence, Desi deep in thought. It made sense that Dorina had been at Hargitay's. With cops banging at Biesu's door, Biesu needed to keep clean. That's why Biesu had Bryony take Dorina to Hargitay, to hide her literally under a cop's nose.

But would Hargitay take Dorina to Biesu now? Desi somehow doubted Hargitay would have the gall to dump Dorina on Biesu's doorstep. Nobody wanted to cross him. Everyone seemed afraid of him. He seemed to have leverage over a lot of people in the form of S&M sex tapes.

And Biesu had a tape of the Hargitays, or at least Deb Hargitay. Maybe the man with the collar that she'd been riding was Al. That was a lot of weight to hold over a cop. Maybe that's how Biesu had bent Hargitay in the first place.

There had to be something else that she wasn't seeing. Then it came to her in a bolt of clarity. That odd moving shadow in the frame of the tape.

"Hey Desi, aren't you getting off at Santa Monica Boulevard?" Fin said.

Desi saw the exit sign. She twisted the wheel and swerved into the off-ramp lane. A car behind them sounded its horn long and hard.

"Hey, I know you're pissed at me, but I don't think I deserve to die," Fin said.

"Not yet, at least," she said.

"Thanks."

She dropped him off in the station parking lot. "You're not coming in?" he said, hand on the door.

"Gotta check out something," she said.

"I guess you're not going to tell me."

"No reason to."

He hesitated, as if hoping she was going to change her mind, then got out of the car. She glanced in the rearview mirror as she exited the lot. His head and shoulders drooped as he strode to the station door.

What the fuck did he want? He should never have come back on the job after that accident. She pushed him out of her mind. She'd deal with him later. She had to get back on the freeway.

20

The scent of blooming roses greeted Desi as she swung her leg over the gate in the picket fence to avoid the creaking hinges. The gauzy light of dawn was starting to filter out the night.

A U-Haul van was parked in the driveway, its rear facing the attached garage as if it were ready to be loaded or unloaded. But the house was quiet, drapes drawn tightly across the front windows.

She jogged across the lawn to the opposite flank of the house where a narrow path led to the back garden. She rounded the corner of the house, drawing her gun and holding it closely across her chest as she moved. Adrenaline sluiced through her veins.

Desi crept to the end of the building and flattening herself against the wall, peeked around the corner. A flagstone patio furnished with a table, chairs, and a gas barbecue fronted a pair of double glass doors.

The view of the interior was shielded by vertical blinds. Off the patio stretched an oblong patch of lawn bordered by more immaculate rose beds.

A muffled scream sounded from the interior of the house. A woman's scream.

Desi crouch-ran to the glass double doors and depressed the handle slowly. It was unlocked.

Pulling it open, she inserted a hand to shunt aside the vertical blinds with a minimum of jangling and crept into a dim dining area. No one was around.

She moved through the dining area into the kitchen. The only sound was the humming of the refrigerator. Then an agonized cry pierced the air.

It was coming from a doorway off the kitchen. She sidled along the wall and twisted the knob. Blood sang in her ears. The door opened on to a flight of stairs leading to a basement. A bleach-white light shone from below.

The sharp report cracked her eardrums, followed by a drawn out cry.

Dorina.

"Where are the DVDs? Tell us and we'll let you go." A woman's gravel voice. Bryony Podeswa.

Desi stepped onto the first step then she felt a crash on the back of her head. Her legs turned into noodles as her Glock clattered somewhere in the distance. Her vision blurred and she crumpled, skidding down several steps.

Desi's eyelids fluttered open to a field of blurry grey stripes behind which shone a blinding light. She closed her eyes, reopened and gained focus. Bars. Metal. She was in a ... cage?

A pain shot through the back of her skull as she tried to lift her head.

She searched her surroundings with her eyes. A bright light on a stand illuminated an old-fashioned torture instrument of a rack. Bound to rollers at each end with coarse rope around her ankles and wrists lay a naked waif of a woman, muddy red streaks and blackish blue marks stippling her pale skin.

Her hair matted with what looked to be mud, or maybe it was excrement. Dorina. Was she dead?

A woman, presumably Bryony, garbed in a dominatrix outfit and a black executioner's hood, stood at the winch at the head of the rack.

A man wearing a black leather harness outfit stood at the foot in shadows.

The eye of a video camera on a tripod aimed out of the darkness at them. On the far side of the room stood a large cage, its door ajar, with two pet food bowls on its floor.

"Again!" the man ordered. Harris Feldman.

Bryony tightened the winch, stretching Dorina's extended arms above her head.

She grimaced and whimpered. She was alive, although barely.

Desi tried to think, but amid the throbs of pain reverberating in her head and the light drilling into every crack of space around her eyes, it was difficult to catch her thoughts and form them into a coherent sequence.

Her head swooned. She squeezed her eyes shut to concentrate on blocking out the world and gaining purchase on her mind. Voices and sounds swam in and out. Then her mind started to clear, and words made sense.

"... still gonna go to that island near India?" Bryony said.

"The plan's still the same but we're going to have to move everything up and just leave everything as is. It's not how I wanted it, but we have no choice. We'll get the first flight out of the country then head to the Maldives," Feldman said.

"They got internet, right?"

"They got it, believe me. We'll still be raking in cash, and nobody will be able to track where we are. Do we have enough footage?"

"Yeah, we got plenty. It's good stuff. We can get a great price for it," Bryony said.

"We'll take it with us. We'll be able to upload it from wherever we're at," Feldman said. "Let's get her and the cop loaded into the truck. We'll leave the bodies at his place. That way everything will point to him. You got the code to get in, right?"

"Yeah, and the key. I can't wait to see him go down for this after the shit he pulled on me, and on you, Harry. He's screwed you out of so much money. What about the DVDs? She said something about 'lawyer.' You think she's contacted a lawyer?"

"Forget about it. The DVDs don't matter now. We don't have time to find them, and we got enough here to make a small fortune. We'll be long gone. Let's go. We gotta move before he gets back. We'll head straight from his place to the airport."

Desi picked up her head. An earthquake of pain resonated through her cranium. A brilliant white light blindsided her. She shielded her eyes with her forearm.

"So detective, you've come to play." Feldman's voice emerged from the blasting light. "I wonder if we should let you into our game."

Feldman chuckled. "What do you think, Mistress?"

"Why not?"

"It would certainly give a new meaning to police brutality." He laughed. "I like it. I like it a lot. In fact, that should be the title."

"The Russians and Japanese will love it," Bryony said. "It'll be a bestseller."

"Too bad we don't have a police uniform. That would make it even better," Feldman said.

"We can get one," Bryony added in a helpful tone.

"No time. By the way, Detective," Feldman said, "I have your phone in case you're looking for it."

Footsteps shuffled up the steps. Desi heard rope slaps and groans and then a grunt of exertion.

Biesu. They were going to take her and Dorina to Biesu's house to frame him.

"Jesus," Bryony muttered.

It was Feldman who left. Bryony must've untied Dorina and was lifting her off the rack.

She heard a dragging sound. Bryony was pulling Dorina across the floor.

Desi edged toward the front of the cage again, wishing they'd turn off that light, and put her mouth to the bars.

"Bryony, don't listen to Feldman. He'll double-cross you just like he's doing to Biesu. He doesn't care about you, only himself."

"Shut up. What the fuck do you know?"

"I know that you've been used and exploited by men your whole life. And I know exactly where the DVDs are. I have them at the police station."

"Yeah, right."

She seemed to be listening. Desi pressed on. "Dorina gave them to Sterling Parker. I found them at his apartment. Help me get Biesu and you can help yourself. Feldman's money isn't going to be enough for both of you forever. He's going to get greedy and want to make another snuff movie, and guess who's going to get the starring role?"

"Biesu tried to fuck me over. He wanted me to take the fall for that asshole who liked being burned. Harry's always been there for me. He'd never do anything to hurt me. You think you know everything, but you don't know nothing, bitch."

Bryony resumed dragging Dorina's inert body up the stairs, huffing and puffing.

Desi slumped in defeat, her head pounding. But amid the throbs, Bryony's words echoed in her brain: "The Russians and Japanese will love it."

Now she knew how Biesu had made his money. He'd been selling the tapes of the BDSM sessions on the dark web, likely without the Thanatos members' consent, and was paid in monero. That was his real business.

Fin sat at his desk, wondering whether he should start clearing it out so he could make a quick getaway when the shit came down. The humiliation of returning to his desk at Newton after he was placed on indefinite administrative leave still burned in his brain.

He didn't see any way that Desi wouldn't rat him out to the lieutenant, not that he blamed her. Maybe he should just resign, save a shred of the little dignity that he had left. He opened the drawers. He actually didn't have anything to clear out since he hadn't even lasted a week. Hardly enough time to accumulate desk junk. That must be some kind of record.

He settled back in his chair. Where the fuck had Desi gone? She'd been deep in thought on the freeway. Then again, what did it matter now? He was off the case and likely off the department. He needed to busy himself with something else.

He picked up the file of the old 7-Eleven armed robbery he'd started to work several days ago. If he could make headway on it, it would give him one small credit. He called up the statewide crime database to look for robberies with similar MOs, but curiosity about Desi's whereabouts gnawed at him. He couldn't concentrate on a pair of scumbags jacking eighty bucks and a handful of gummy bears.

He got up and walked to her desk, scanning it for clues. Sterling Parker's DVDs were open on her desk, one of them was empty.

She'd been watching them. He should've thought of that. He sat and pressed a key on her keyboard.

A scene out of a medieval torture chamber mushroomed on the computer screen. A man, naked except for a blindfold, knelt on the floor, his wrists manacled to chains on the wall. He was being lashed with a whip. The camera zoomed in on the stripes of flayed red flesh. It was real. Fin's stomach seesawed.

Then he saw it.

The point of a cat's tail, the color of burnt gold, slipped off the edge of the screen.

He knew where Desi had gone, and she was fucking crazy to go there herself. He grabbed his jacket.

21

Curling her back to the fierce light, Desi listened to the rhythmic bumping of Bryony heaving Dorina up the stairs. The sounds stopped. She must have reached the top. Desi was now alone in the basement.

She rattled one of the bars to test the strength of the cage. It was made of lightweight metal, designed for use in sex games not for keeping captives.

The light behind her cast an elongated shadow of the cage bars on the wall and what looked like a stack of kitchen chairs. And something else under the chairs. Odd shaped.

Her Glock.

Hope surged. Was it close enough to reach? It was hard to tell with the distorted shape of shadows.

She edged toward the side of the cage making the shadows, lay on her back and wiggled her arm through the bars up to her armpit.

She could just reach the leg of the bottom chair.

She strained against the bar as hard as she could to gain a smidgen more length. Her weight against the bars tilted the cage a fraction, but she was still at least several inches short of the gun. Fuck.

She lay back. The cage had budged. She rolled her full body weight against the side of the cage. It rocked. She rolled back a little further and again slammed her body into the side of the cage.

It tipped, with the upper edge landing on top of the stacked chairs. The upside-down legs of the chair protruded through the cage.

The gun was almost under her. She snaked her arm through the bars on the side resting on the chairs and patted around for it. Her fingers could just reach the butt. She scrabbled for it, but her anxious grasping nudged the gun a fraction of an inch away.

Fuck. She had to relax, take her time. Which she didn't have. Footsteps thumped overhead. They'd be back in the basement at any moment.

Again, she lay against the bottom side of the cage and extended her arm through, patting the floor for the gun. Her fingertips caught the textured surface of the butt. She pawed it toward her, bit by bit.

The door opened. The staircase creaked. Sweat sprouted on her forehead. Just a tad more then she'd be able to fully grasp it. The footsteps were almost at the bottom of the stairs.

Desi slid the gun closer. Then her fingers curled around the butt. She snatched it and stuck it in her jacket pocket as footsteps halted behind the upturned cage.

"What the fuck is this? Attempted jailbreak?" Bryony barked a laugh.

Desi didn't respond. She lurched as Bryony pulled the cage down from the tilt. It landed on the floor with a thunk and a bright blast of light. She kept her arm pressed against the gun in her pocket to disguise the bulge.

Bryony switched off the movie lamp, leaving a dim-light from a ceiling fixture. Desi's eyes felt immediate relief.

Bryony stood in front of the cage with a pair of handcuffs swinging from a hand like a pendulum.

"Turn around with your back to the door and put your hands behind your back," Bryony said.

Desi did as she was told. The door creaked open behind her, and Bryony grabbed one of her wrists, which meant she was right behind her. Desi kicked her right leg backward as hard as she could.

It connected with a plate of bone. Bryony yelped, slightly loosening her grip on Desi's wrist. Desi yanked her arm free, spinning around as she pulled out her gun. She trained it with both hands at Bryony's chest.

"Hands on your head. Now!"

"Fuck you!" Bryony dropped the handcuffs and laced her fingers on top of her head.

"Turn around, slowly."

Bryony shuffled so her back was facing Desi. The detective bent her legs to sweep up the manacles with one hand, keeping the Glock and her eyes aimed at Bryony's back.

She cocked one handcuff open and clicked it around one of Bryony's wrists, then deftly fastened the other and lowered the pair of manacled hands.

Desi shoved the nine-millimeter's nose in the small of Bryony's back. "Where's Feldman?" she hissed into her ear.

"Loading the van."

"Where's my phone?"

"Harris has it."

"Up the stairs! Go! Say one word and I'll shoot."

They marched up the stairs. When they reached the top step, Desi clenched Bryony's upper arm, pushing her into a stagger down the hall as she held her tightly against her body like a shield. She had to get out of the house, get to her car.

The overwhelming silence of the house pricked her senses into high alert. It was too quiet. Then she felt something against the back of her head. Small, cold, hard. She halted in midstride, her nerves jangling.

With a borrowed blue bubble light stuck onto the SUV's dashboard that parted freeway traffic like the Red Sea, Fin pulled into the street and cruised slowly by Harris Feldman's house. The garage door was rolled up, revealing the nose of a van backed in, as if getting ready to leave. The empty Crown Vic was parked a house down from Feldman's.

He was right. This was where Desi had come.

He swung a U-turn at the end of the street and stopped. Fin called his partner's cell. It went straight to voicemail. She must be inside. He was going to have to go in.

He took a deep breath, held it for a count of three, then exhaled. He had to think rationally. He couldn't let his reflexes trip him up as they had before. All the rules he had violated scrolled through his mind.

Number one: Call for backup.

He reached for his phone and requested additional units. He hung up and then he saw it. Every nerve cell in his body sparked into flame. His palms slid on the wheel as if they were greased. His breathing grew quick and short.

He couldn't wait.

"Drop the gun, Detective," Harris Feldman said, poking the muzzle of a handgun into her skull with some force.

Desi let her nine-millimeter clang to the wooden floor and raised her hands. Bryony, freed from her captor's clench, wheeled and placed a forceful kick to her crotch. Desi jack-knifed, her eyes watering with the jolt of pain.

"How does it feel, bitch?" Bryony said.

Annoyance crossed Feldman's face. "Shut up and move the hell out of the way. Jesus, you get on my nerves sometimes."

"I need the cuff keys," she said.

"Hold on. I have to cuff her first." He jabbed Desi's head with the gun. "Walk." She obeyed. He marched her into the kitchen and through a side door into the garage where the van's rear yawned wide open.

Feldman grabbed another pair of handcuffs from a box, clicked them around her wrists and ordered her to get in the van.

Desi climbed in. Dorina lay still amid several bags and suitcases with a sheet covering her. The doors slammed shut, and darkness dropped like a curtain. Desi felt for Dorina's pulse. It was faint, but there.

She looked around, her eyes adjusting to blackness. A panel walled off the rear of the vehicle from the front seats and the rear door windows were blacked out. It was a perfect rapist's van.

A minute later the garage door screeched. The front doors of the van opened, and Feldman and Bryony jumped into the seats. The engine started. The van lurched forward.

Desi concentrated, tracking the van's progress in her head. It slowed. They had reached the end of the driveway. A bump. She rolled. They had turned into the street.

The van pulled out of the driveway. Feldman was at the wheel and Bryony Podeswa rode shotgun. The van moved away from Fin down the street. They hadn't noticed him.

Beads of sweat dribbled down his temples. He twisted his fists around the wheel. He had to do this. He couldn't let them get away. Not this time. He stamped the gas pedal.

Fin zoomed alongside the van, overtaking it, then he yanked the wheel to the left and hit the brakes at the same time, cutting off Feldman's van with a squeal of rubber and a jolt.

Feldman jammed into the rear fender of Fin's SUV. The van's airbags deployed, filling the front seats with puffy white clouds.

Fin leapt out of the car and drew his weapon, pointing it at Feldman, who was batting down the bags to keep from being smothered.

"Where are they?" Fin yelled.

He didn't wait for an answer. He raced to the back of the van and pulled open the doors. Desi blinked, stunned. She recovered and scrambled out.

Fin grabbed her arm. "You okay?"

"Call for an RA. Dorina's in bad shape," she said. "I'm okay."

"Get Bryony, I'll get Feldman," he said.

They hauled out Podeswa and Feldman and had them lie face down in the street. Fin cuffed them.

Desi rubbed her head and looked around. Fin's car was a diagonal slash in the front of the van. Fin could see her figuring out what had happened.

She looked at him. "And you? You okay?"

He jughandled his hands on his hips. "I'm okay."

The sound of yelping sirens blasted the air.

22

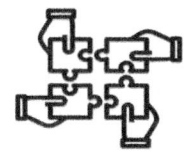

The sun was sliding into the horizon, etching the sky with strokes of crimson. Fin clicked off the cell phone and set it next to him on the beach. He glanced out at the sea and continued moving his pencil over the sketch pad. The outline of a surfer riding the waves emerged on the page.

Desi rode into shore and hopped off the board, grabbing it as she waded out of the ocean. She jogged up the beach and collapsed on the sand next to Fin. He showed her the latest sketch.

"That's good," she said.

"Not bad for a moving target in low light."

"More than not bad," she said. "Can I have it when you're done?"

"I'm going to use it as the outline for a painting, but the painting is for you."

"Really?" she said

"I owe you. Hey, the DA just called. With the DNA positive for Dorina's sister, they're adding another count of murder on Biesu, Feldman, and Podeswa. It looks like Bryony's going to cut a deal and testify against Biesu and Feldman, and they're going to get the crime victim visa for Dorina. She's still in the hospital. The IRS is also sniffing around Biesu so he may have some hefty tax bills to pay."

"I'm glad, most of all for Dorina," Desi said.

Fin added more details to the sketch.

"You still want to promote to RHD?" she asked.

He kept moving the pencil, adding a shadow. "You know what? I think I'm good right where I am. I'm putting the house on the market and moving out here. But you should take the Hollywood job."

She stared at the horizon. The bright coin of the sun was descending fast.

"You heard it all in the parking lot, I take it."

"I gather Nichols was the reason you left Hollywood."

"His wife found out about our affair and complained to the captain. Then Nichols hit me with a sexual harassment beef. To make it go away, I took a transfer to West LA."

"If he's not going to be there anymore, you should go for Hollywood. You have this going for you, too." He put down the pencil, picked up his phone and handed it to Desi.

The screen held a Times story that had just been posted about the arrests of Biesu, Feldman, and Podeswa.

"Read the whole thing later. Just check out the last paragraph," he said.

Desi scrolled down. "Detective Desi Nimmo led the investigation," she read aloud. She smiled. "It was you who tipped off the media, wasn't it?" she said, putting down the phone.

"Guilty as charged. I also called the reporter earlier today and made sure your name got mentioned. I'm guilty of a lot of things."

Her phone buzzed with a text. Denny.

Now a good time for that rain check?

She smiled. Then an idea flashed into her head.

It's good. Can we do a quick moving job with your truck first?

Sure.

Desi stood up, brushing sand off the seat of her wetsuit.

"You going already?" Fin said.

"I got an errand to do."

An hour and a half later, she walked into the West LA branch library. She spotted him leaning into a computer booth.

"Sal," she stage-whispered.

He looked around and pursed his lips in distaste when he saw her before turning back to the monitor.

"I got a surprise for you. In the alley," she said.

"What? Steel bracelets with a nice little chain? Or a card that says, 'Go directly to jail. Do not pass go. Do not collect $200'?"

"Just come check it out."

"If I get up now, I'll lose my spot."

"Suit yourself."

Desi walked out of the library and crossed Santa Monica Boulevard to the alley, where she waited in the alcove of the coffee shop's rear door. Several minutes later, Sal turned the corner.

He stopped as he spotted the burgundy velvet couch that she and Denny had just picked up from Brentwood and unloaded in the alley. Then he barreled toward it like a torpedo. He stopped in front of it, stroked the velvet as if it would purr, then flopped on it with gusto, hands clasped behind his head.

Desi smiled. She pushed open the coffee shop door, walked through and exited onto the street where Denny was waiting in his truck parked at the curb.

"All good?" he said as she climbed in.

"All good.

About the Author

Christina Hoag is a former journalist who has had her laptop searched by Colombian guerrillas, phone tapped in Venezuela, was suspected of drug trafficking in Guyana, hid under a car to evade Guatemalan soldiers, and posed as a nun to get inside a Caracas jail. She has interviewed gang members, bank robbers, thieves and thugs in prisons, shantytowns and slums, not to forget billionaires and presidents, some of whom fall into the previous categories. Now she writes about such characters in her fiction.

She has had numerous short stories, creative nonfiction essays and poems published in anthologies and literary journals and has won several awards.

She's a former staff writer for the Miami Herald and Associated Press and reported from fourteen countries around Latin America for Time, Business Week, New York Times, Financial Times, Sunday Times of London, Houston Chronicle and other news outlets.

Born in New Zealand, Christina grew up as an expat in seven countries, arriving in the United States as a teenager. She now lives in California, where she has taught creative writing at a maximum-security prison and to at-risk teen girls.

If you liked this book, please help spread the word and leave a review or rating on Amazon or other book review sites.

The author is available for speaking engagements at writing conferences and groups, book clubs, bookstores, and libraries.

Sign up for her newsletter at:

https://ChristinaHoag.com

Follow her on social media:

Twitter: @ChristinaHoag
Instagram: @ChristinaHoagAuthor
Facebook: ChristinaHoag

Read her essays, short stories and articles at:

Medium.com/@ChristinaHoag

Printed in Great Britain
by Amazon